Best Relationship Ever

Aayush Verma

MORE BY **AAYUSH VERMA**

Student Life = friends + love + family + school

Dear Daddy

Invincible Love

Best Relationship Ever

Aayush Verma

BEST RELATIONSHIP EVER

First Edition – 22nd September 2016

Second Edition – 17th July 2018

This book is a work of fiction. None of the contents and characters mentioned in the book is real and based on true incidents. All the names, places and incidents are used fictionally and it is a part of Author's imagination. Any resemblance to person living or dead is purely coincidental. This book is not against any community and religious beliefs.

Promoted and Marketed by: Knack Ardour

ISBN: 978-81-933783-1-1

From the Author

Dear Readers,

Thank you for choosing "Best Relationship Ever" (second part of the series: Student Life).This novel is all about two teenage couples Abhijeet & Anamika and their life. They love each other much more than any other person but yet there is something which makes them go far from each other time to time.

They manage to live peacefully together by going hand in hand with each other.

In between their unique relationship, they had to manage the things happening with them but they never stopped loving each other and getting away from each there. They simply worked on to save their relationship and some other things with this like friends, family, study, exams and more.

This book is not only related with the love of two common teenagers but it also related with something too much far from that. It is related with life, the life of Abhijeet and Anamika which reflects the identity of every teenage love couples's life.

It is something which can make any sad person to enjoy his life. In spite of having a true love story and best relationship of Abhijeet and Anamika, there is a lot to know about much more than this.

It was really impossible for me to write about the Second Part of Student Life, but the love and support from the friends and readers like you had made be able to do so. I would really like to thank some of my near ones who supported me in creating the possibilities. A great thanks to the awesome friend Sanjana Gupta for encouraging and supporting me towards the very beginning.

The supporting roles of my buddies Puja, Abhay and Aditi are really appreciative.

With thanks to our team at Knack Ardour, and including everyone who contributed their efforts towards the making of this book. And most importantly, a huge thanks to our happy readers like you! You guys mean a lot to me.

Please mail us your feedback and suggestions at aayushvermaofficial@gmail.com. I will be looking forward for your feedback.

I hope you find this book helpful, best of luck for your life.

Happy Reading!!

With lots of love,

Aayush Verma

There is so much to share with you,

Please do visit: facebook.com/narratordesk

*****TO EVERYONE WHO VALUE THE TRUE AND SWEETEST PART OF LIFE*****

Chapter 1

So it's all about priorities. Sometimes, we cannot live without friends and sometimes we leave our circles just to greet our new relationship companion. Our choices and priorities changes as we grow up.

Such a change happened with us when our Happy Buddies group broke into pieces. All the members were occupied to make a happy ship except me and Anurag. In the way of making up a happy ship, they left out our circle. Only Anurag is the one still together with me.

So this friendship group was broken down and a new group was formed including Me, Anurag, Anamika and Nandini (Anurag's Girlfriend).

Nandini was the same girl for which Anurag had a crush on. He found her luckily on Facebook few months before and with this interaction with her, he also came to know about the un-conditional love and sacrifices what she did for him.

It was a bad moment that they both got separated and Nandini was sent to another city. But, now as she came back, what not happened in past is happening now. Both are tagged together in the bonds of relationship.

On the other side, my bonding with Anamika is becoming stronger and stronger.

Though we are not having much interaction because of the examination, but it doesn't mean we are out of relationship. This

Valentines we have decided to sacrifice our time and meet with each other.

It's already been a month since the last meeting, so we both were excited for the very coming day. It was a sudden plan we just came forward in between the examination.

The Valentine's Day

"It's too crowded here", said Anamika.

"Yes, dear and why not it will be? It's a valentine week".

"Yeah, and it's our first valentine together".

"So?"

"We must be celebrating together".

"Are we separated?"

"No, but let's not feel like being separated?".

"If you are saying this because of last week, then I'm sorry, I was too engaged with school stuffs that time".

"So kind of busy that you don't have time to talk with your girlfriend?"

"I'm sorry. Next time, I'll never ignore you".

"OK, fine now".

"Thanks for understanding. It's so sweet of you".

"Ha-ha. Why are you talking like a girl?"

"I was just doing your acting".

"Oho, stop it otherwise I'll not decorate your assignment".

"A very big deal, my hands are up, sorry", I said, kidding.

(She came closer and pulled my cheek).

"Hey, I am not your toy", I said destroying her curly hair, which was attached in a proper way with the help of 4-5 hair clips.

"For your info, we are at Ambaar Campus".

"Yes, we are. So?"

"Many people are present here".

"I don't care about these people and their negative thoughts, what I care is how we think about each other".

"Yeah, right and you know what whenever I meet you... I really.... really feel very happy".

"And if I meet you then I have no idea that how fast the time gets finished. I enjoy our every moment".

"And really it's with me also".

"The so much similar we are, seems like we are made for each other only".

"Yeah, and that's why we understand and fill each other problems in a much better way than the other".

(The waiter came in between our conversation).

"Sir, would you like to have a Valentine's Special cake in place of the black forest cake? It had been especially designed for this week only", said the waiter.

"Yes, sure, but bring it faster".

"Hmmm. Valentine's Special cake, sounds good"

"Yes, dear, let's have a special cake in this special time. Do you have any problem?"

"Noah, it's great".

"Yeah, it is. Can you please see the 3rd Row, 2nd table?

"Yes, (after looking) Oh, my God, it's Anurag".

"And don't forget to look after that girl, it's her girlfriend, so beautiful".

"Wow, see what a handsome guy he is!!"

"Who?", I asked, looking here and there.

"The guy sitting behind the next table"

"Yes, he is, mind it, he has his girlfriend and you have your boyfriend".

"You also focus on this. You also had a girlfriend and that girl also had a boyfriend".

"I was just checking you, but as I know nobody is more beautiful than my own girlfriend".

"Alright, alright, fine now".

(After a pause)

"Abhijeet, if you don't mind then can we call both of them to join us?"

"Yeah, why not?"

"Then take out your phone and call him".

(In between, the waiter came back with cake).

"Sir, your cake. Anything else, Sir?"

"Not right now. We'll call you if we need something".

"Sure, thank you Sir", said he.

(Waiter left, I took out my phone and called Anurag).

"Hey there. Where are you?"

"Hey bro, I am in Ambaar, hanging out with my girlfriend. If there is no any urgent matter, then can we talk later?"

"I and Anamika are also in the same restaurant in which you are dating with her".

"You and Anamika?? Really? "

"Yes, would you like to join us?"

"Yes bro, but why hadn't you told me about this planning?"

"See, anything was not pre-planned, we find time and came together".

"Yup. Wait, I'm coming".

(Anurag drops the call and came soon after that).

"Hello friends."

"Hi, how are you and your girlfriend?", I said.

"She's pretty fine. What about you guys?"

"We are also fine. So how's your first party going on with her?", asked Anamika.

"In an awesome way, buddy".

"From how many hour are you here?", I asked.

"Two hours, what about you guys?"

"From one hour only", I said.

"But Anurag, you hadn't told us about this event with your girlfriend?", asked Anamika.

"Actually, everything happened so fast that I forgot to tell you guys, in fact, I hadn't told anybody about this".

"So is it over now?"

"Yes, can we get arranged in the same table?"

"Yeah, yeah, why not?", I said.

"Thanks, I'm coming in 10 minutes with her, till then you guys have your personal talks", said Anurag and left.

"Abhijeet, you are the first boyfriend of my life and I wanted you to remain the same for forever".

"I promise, wish we had met before I met Akshita".

"Hmm, but what's problem with now?"

"No problem, just lucky to have you ".

"I love you ".

"I love you much more than the three words can say".

(Comes closer and kisses me on the cheek with wrapping her hand on my shoulder).

"Lovely".

"Now take out handkerchief and rub the symbol printed on your cheeks".

(Doing the same)

"But I can't rub what's printed in my heart ".

"A place had already been permanently reserved in my heart for forever".

"Really? So tell me from which day this space had been created in your heart?"

"From the very first meeting only"

"But I came to know about this in December ".

"Yeah, just because you were busy with Akshita ".

"She hadn't any good turns with me as I have with you, so just I'm happy she left me and much happier with your entrance in my life as a girlfriend ".

(Anamika was there to say something, but suddenly Anurag came with his girlfriend).

"Hello guys, this is Nandini and Nandini this is Anamika (Both said Hello to each other and shook hands together) and he's Abhijeet", Anurag introduced us ".

"Hello Abhijeet ", she said.

"Hello. Have a seat here ".

"Thanks Abhijeet and Anamika it's nice to meet you guys, I had heard a lot about both of you".

"Nice to meet you also, Nandini", we said, together.

"You both are really looking fabulous together ".

"Thanks, you both are also a great match together", said Anamika.

"Thank you, Anamika", she said.

"Friends, can we have a photograph together?", Anurag asked.

"Yeah, but who will take?", Anamika said.

(Everybody became blanked).

"The waiter", I said after a while.

"His work is to serve foods, not of taking photographs",Nandini said.

"You just wait".

(I pressed the call bell button).

"Yes Sir", said the waiter who just came after a few seconds.

"Can you please manage our photographs together?", I asked while taking out the mobile phone to give him.

"Sure, Sir", says he (smiling) and takes the phone.

(After taking four -five pictures)

"Please move a bit closer to each other", said the waiter to us.

We did the same, after that he came and said", Sir, is this okay? (Showing the photo)?"

"It's not just okay, it's wonderful", I said.

"Thank you, Sir. Any more things needed?"

"Bring two more plates as you see two more of my circle joined us".

"No problem Sir, I'll be back, shortly ".

"So, Anurag?"

"Yes bro".

"You still have a patch up party debt ".

"I know, bro, I'll clear it just after exam".

"Ahem. Ahem. We both will clear it, as it's our patch up party, not only yours", said Nandini.

"Oh, very good", Anamika said.

"Thank you, Anamika".

"Alright, if both of you don't mind then can we go to a closer place?", asked Anurag.

"Yeah, no problem, but try coming soon", Nandini said.

"We will shortly come".

(After coming out of the restaurant, we went inside cold drink corner and ordered two small cans of Coca- cola which came soon after our order as there was not much crowd in the shop).

"So Abhijeet, how's your life going with Anamika?"

"It's going better what about your life with Nandini?"

"Running smoothly, you know I don't want to come here, but due to Nandini's wish I had to ".

"As examination days are coming closer, we all are tense, but having a hangout with them is also important, also whenever we met them our pains gets disappeared".

"Yes, I agree with all these words, I would like to say that our girls are best for us".

"But we also need to be the best for them, as it is the first valentine together so we must not hurt their wishes".

"Yup, right said bro, but in this matter, I hurt her lot, man. From the first day of the previous week, she was requesting me to go to this event and each time I hurt her by saying NO".

"But now, as you both are together, so had you enjoyed the first party in this valentine week with her?"

"Yes, I feel like I am a free parrot tonight, but again we all are going to be caged at home to prepare for exams, anyways something good between you and Anamika?".

"We are perfect in ourselves and our relationship so everything is good between us".

"Great, and bro, let's go now before they call us".

"Yeah, let's go".

We finished our cold drink and escaped to the restaurant.

(After reaching, we saw both of them were so busy in their gossips that they hadn't noticed us. We shifted to the side and started listening to them as that was the only thing we can do).

"Anamika, you know them from before, so tell me of how many years are our boyfriends together with each other as best friends?"

"They are together before my coming only, so no idea how much older is their friendship ".

"Ok, leave it, but see both of them are quite similar in their talking and behaviour ".

"Yeah, right, both are them are a similar kind of duffers".

"But, still they are our duffer only, not of anybody else.

"Yes Nandini, you are right".

"So what discussion is going on between both of the birds?", I asked, hiding what we have heard.

"Oh, you guys are back", Nandini said.

"Yes, so what was going on?", Anurag asked.

"Nothing, just having some personal talks", Nandini said.

"Became so personal in just 20 minutes?", I asked.

"Dude, don't you know that our girls are extra special of a kind".

"Yes, point to be noted",.

"Do you guys having any problem with us?", Anamika asked.

"We had never poked between both of your friendship, then why are you?", Nandini said.

"No, no, why we will have problems, in fact, we all are a company", Anurag said.

"Yes, we are a company of unique friends and unique couples. And Anurag, let's make this company alive forever, what's your decision? ".

"If our girls support and co-operate us, then why not?"

"Had we said No?", Nandani asked.

"But you haven't said yes also", Anurag replied.

"Tangled in between yes and no", I said.

"Yes, we will", said both together.

"Yeah, thanks, Abhijeet it's 6:30PM, so let's get finished with our eatables, we can manage our late but girls can't ".

"Yes, right".

We arranged those eatables and ate them within ten minutes.

Anurag and Nandini started to leave as both of them had their homes far off.

"Thanks for this great time, guys", Nandini said.

"Mention not. You are also a part of us now", said Anamika.

"Let's see when we are going to meet again. Bye Anamika ".

"We'll meet in the classroom tomorrow, bye Abhijeet", Anurag said.

(After Anurag and Nandini left)

"So what personal talk was going on when we were outside?"

“Is it necessary to know?”

“In case if it is not so deeply personal”.

“It’s very deeply personal”, she said (smiling).

“Ok, no problem”.

“Hmm. Dear, I think it's time to move to our homes. What about some almond chocolates at the end?”

“Yeah, sure”.

(The waiter was called and ordered the same).

In the way to Anamika’s home:

“I enjoyed every part of tonight and all the credit goes to you. If you were not in my life, then it remained like black & white picture”, I said.

“Don’t say like that, even I’m lucky to have a charm in my life”.

“Hey, I’m not a lucky charm (wait) why there is sadness in a beautiful face?”

“I don’t know when we’ll meet next. I really miss you and this day”.

“Sadly, I also don’t know about this, but dear, why are you worried about the next meeting? Do you think I’ll leave you? And listen you are my lucky charm, not I”.

“No, you are my lucky charm”.

“We both are each other’s charm”.

“We’ll go holding each other’s hand in the road of life, together forever”

"I promise, till we are alive, we'll be together".

(She came and hugged me. I hugged her tighter)

"Now I am comfortable".

"I'm also", I said.

(Pulls my cheeks, I did the same)

"You are my lovely and beautiful princess".

"And you are my cute and naughty prince".

"Beautiful kiddy princess".

"Cute lovely charm".

(Kisses on the lips)

"I love you", said she.

"How many times you will say this?"

"I will say it whenever I feel like. By the way, is this my reply? Don't you love me?"

"I love you much more than the ones who repeat it twenty times a day".

(Long kissed her)

"That was WONDERFULLL".

"Thanks. Dear, it's the time to say bye now".

"Yes, Abhijeet. I think we'll meet after exam only?"

"Hmmm, but I wished that we should spend 14th February together".

"Next year we will be celebrating together".

"If you will be together, then only"

(Hits slightly on the shoulder)

"When the girls find a perfect guy than his present boyfriend, then they spent no time in leaving them".

"I don't know why you think like a stupid".

"Akshita also says like that way, but everybody knows what happened at the end. She left me".

"Don't compare me with Akshita", she warned me.

"I was just kidding you. The truth can be seen in the eyes".

"But whenever you talk like this way, I become worried and exhausted. These words show lack of trust, whatever it was a joke or anything, don't repeat it again".

"You are right. Next time, I'll never repeat it".

"Okay,(after a few seconds) Stop here now, my home is near only".

"Wait, may I expect one more stamp on the lips?"

"No", she replied.

"When I ask you, you say no and when I don't ask you then I get a best one. What's reason behind this?"

"Whenever you will ask I'll say 'No'. You don't need to ask your girlfriend about this. Do you understand?"

"Mmmhmmm".

(*********)

“Bye, my prince”.

“Bye, lovely princess”.

(Text arrived on the phone, after moving few distance apart)

Anamika: How was that?

Abhijeet: A memorior. We will get in touch after month only”.

Anamika: I’ll miss you.

Abhijeet: Miss you too. I’ll talk after reaching home. Take care, bye .

(After texting her, I kept my hone on the pocket and resumed riding towards home).

Chapter 2

21st February

Just after a week of the meeting, we have decided to meet together and visit the Local Temple before the beginning of the examination.

Anamika was worried and blanked. I was much worried because of this.

She was very much confused and disturbed with her life. Her closer family members made a pre pressure on her regarding the examination. This time they wanted her to score the higher as the previous one was not up to the mark.

Whenever we face the problems in life or go through hard times, there's only one way to increase confidence and willingness to work hard for achieving something better in life. The way is to follow up the Supreme Power which we call God and that's why we planned to visit a temple.

The pleasant environment and the silence inside the temple made us feel powerful and motivated. We both stepped together inside the campus of the Krishna temple.

A group of monks were present inside the temple. They were enjoying in their own moods chanting the name of the Lord. Some of them were describing the Power of Spirituality and God among all the visitors inside the temple.

They say that in this Yuga, we only look forward to the material interests and monetary benefits. The pillars of a relationship are not connected with reality but with some of the material interests.

Because of this material interests, we commit a lot of crimes, we are in the web of our mind which always tells us to do which always makes us commit the wrong things which gives us fast comfort. When our choices and material interests change, we end up of our bonds of relationship or personal belongingness.

We were totally dissolved in the positive environment and positive thoughts. Some monks noticed us being blanked and worried. They walked and greeted with us. They said that they are monks travelling to all the corners of the world to help people with living a beautiful life and maintain a strong bond.

It's really interesting to meet with someone who left the charm and happiness of this world just to follow up the Path of Supreme Power. He asked us if we can give him some minutes.

"Off course", we said.

He made us sit on the clean marble floor. Both of us were silent. The monks started up the conversation.

"So, you guys are brothers and sisters, Right?"

"No, we study in the same class".

"So ,classmates? Friends?"

"They must be in a relationship", another monk said.

"How can you understand this?"

"I just guessed that"

"Okay, let's come towards the Karma and the Problems of Life. Do you guys know about the actions or incidents which happen around us?"

"Yes, we have turned out to be more selfish and criminal kind of. A real sacrifice, love and care are declining among us. We do harm and hurt the animals as well", Anamika said.

"This is one of things but not the major one. The main thing happening in this world is that we are giving more priorities to the material things and short term happiness and because of this, our each and everything is getting worse. Crime and Selfishness are the outcomes of these happenings. Faith, trust and relationships with God and humans is slowing down".

"But is there anything that can save us from these outcomes?"

"Yes, it is and that's why we are here. We travel to different places for creating awareness among the people to follow the path of the God and get attached with the Higher Level of Power"

"How can we come out of this? Being honest, we were not even much interested with the God?"

"It's not difficult but it's difficult to control the beginning. Following up the Path of God it's a bit difficult but not impossible. One can start stepping from today".

"Do we need to visit up the temples each day and do the fasting?"

"No, this is not it. You do not have to follow up the temple but follow up the words of God. A teacher will not be impressed if you visit up his home daily and do countless sacrifice for him. He will be more than happy if you follow up his advice, methods and do the best in the exam. Here, the life is the exam, Lord as a teacher, and the advices and methods are his words and Principles which we keep spreading through spreading the knowledge and awareness. We also provide free nano books which is packed up with the

Principles to live a happy life, too much far from troubles and cheap works"

"Do you have that nano-booklet? How much it costs?"

"Yes, we do have it and we will give it to you. We do not sell it, we distribute it for free. If you want to make up the cost, then do follow it up in your life".

(One of the monks forwarded us the two booklets).

As they were having a very short time, so they asked if we have something that we are unable to understand.

"How can perform better in our life roles?"

"In order to perform well, you need to focus and work hard. Because, the major Principle is Karma Yoga, you will get only what you deserve by your works. Whether it's maintaining up a relationship from both side co-operation or working and learning, we need to sacrifice something to gain something. Each and everything is easy to maintain and achieve, once we come out of the materials in the materialistic world. We need to come out thinking about the good results without doing anything. We don't deserve to get something good, without doing anything for it. When we come out of the materialistic attractions, we will get higher level of happiness and remain positive even in bad times also. Bad thoughts and hard situations will not break our Positive Attitude. There will be no reaction of bad things on us".

These words made our day and gifted us Positive Motivation at the right time. Anamika was feeling better and she described her feelings like some light enter inside her soul giving higher positive energy. I was feeling like someone came and offered me highly dedicated Motivational drink or syrup which I drank the whole at once.

Chapter 3

The days of the examination are so like the breath taking days of every average student like us. It makes us far from our fun and makes dissolved in books like a book worm.

On the very first day of examination, there were more Parents than students outside the main gate of School Centre. The parents were worried more than the students. In our area, a crowd of people is seen only because of three reasons: 1. Festival, 2. Examination Season and 3. Marriage

All of us were surrounded with too many parents. Anamika's exam centre was also the same as mine. Her Father and Mother both were together with her outside the hall. They were explaining her and motivating her.

Though she was very close to me, but just because of her parents, I was unable to communicate with her, we just had small eye contacts for a second.

Anurag arrived and we walked a shorter distance to find a cool place out of the crowds. A robo book worm came closer to us.

LAST DAY: MATHEMATICS EXAM

A lot of people had reached the exam centre before our arrival. There was a lot of tension reflecting from each other faces.

We were also tensed and why not we will be? It was the mathematics exam (much more difficult than any other subject).

When we all friends met, Avishek (maths master mind) introduced us with some tips and tricks (as promised) to solve maths for achieving good marks. He also explained us by solving the latest CBSE questions (CCE pattern) through two-three ways.

He told us so much that the fear of the examination became forbidden from our mind and that's how we became relaxed (but for a short time only).

After seeing the question paper in the exam hall, our minds got frozen like a curd (in Hindi, we say it "Dimmag ki Dahi").

We were unable to understand what to do, as most of the questions were very much difficult and time taking also.

While deep reading e question paper for 15 minutes, we got some idea and solved the questions in which we were confirmed that we can solve it.

After finishing those questions, we tried solving the questions in which we were less confirmed about finding an exact solution.

The three hard hours got ended so much fast (just like the Science exam),that we had to leave the whole part of 2-4 questions and few parts of some lengthy questions (just because of time shortage and misunderstanding the questions).

(Outside the campus)

Shreyansh: How difficult the paper was!

Anurag: Very difficult bro. Some questions were too hard that I became unable to understand them.

Shreyansh: Have you tried solving them? or not?

Anurag: I had tried, but not became successful and ended up with leaving three questions as no time was available.

Me: I had also left two of the questions.

Avishek: I also had to leave some of it.

Anurag: How can you leave the questions? You're lying. I don't think you have skipped any of the questions.

Avishek: Honestly, I had also left two long questions and one short question.

Anurag: If this is the condition of the topper, then one can understand how hard the question set was!

Avishek: Yeah buddy, leave it. I hope you guys had worked a lot solving out every question with all your potential, in the same way.

Anurag: Yes bro, I have used it. Thanks for that.

Shreyansh: I have, also, but I became unable to solve some questions completely and left the half part of it.

Avishek: Great. And don't worry as there is step marking scheme. Now let us do the overall counting and see how much we are scoring.

Anurag: After two days, we will do that work. I'm tired a lot, need some rest.

(Before we could say something, some of our class friends surrounded us. They had kept packets of colours in their hands, some were burning crackers, all shouting and enjoying).

They all were looking just like the imagination of the Indian citizens celebrating the first Independence Day (15 th August,1947).

And really for us, it was not less than that.

(After years of continuous study in the school, from childhood (Nursery) to now(class 10) was a kind of step by step struggle, but now, we got freedom from junior education. This freedom is of a very short duration (as after that we need to face higher education) but still this freedom means a lot to us or every student of Class 10 who completed the BOARD's exam).

We tried escaping from them (the class friends), but Shreyansh stopped us and that's how we got mixed in that happiness (along with a great sadness that we will not be found together in the school uniform. We will never meet. We will never go n the school where bundles of our memories are stored in every corner of the Missionary School).

They came carrying colours, spread it to our faces, hairs and also on the white uniform. We took group selfie, exchanged contact with every one of them, shared some good moments with each other and then came back happily to our homes.

(At the home)

I pressed the doorbell button.

My small sister came running by.

"Oh my God! Ye kya haal bana liye ho aapna? (What condition have you made of yourself?)Tum Abhijeet bhaiya hi ho na? Ya koi aur?(Are you Abhijeet only or anybody else?", lill sister asked.

"Chup karo, pehle aandar toh aane do ghar mein (Shut up, let me come inside the house)",I said (pulling her cheeks from the half opened door).

(She slammed the door, locked it and went inside without letting me in.(My small sister: Seven years in age, a mixed combo pack of danger, drama, fun, happiness and more things which I can't predict because she can't tolerate a small funny insult by his brother (but she can do and I had to tolerate it) and can strike anytime just like some natural phenomena(earthquakes) and as one knows, these things can't be predicted. Scientists are still working on that).

I pressed the doorbell again and this time, my elder brother came.

"Enjoyed a lot with with friends?", he asked.

"Yes, some class friends came and we had to join them as that was the last moment of interaction with them".

"Ok, nice. Come inside", he said.

When I came inside, I saw my small sister standing like an angry bodyguard (just looking like a red tomato).

“I’m sorry”, I said (to her).

“Rakho tum aapna sorry aapne pass, mere homework me help kaar dena, evening me market chalna saath mein,or haan ek baat aur thi but woh to mein bhul hi gayi (Keep your sorry with yourself, but in return, help me in my homeworks, we will go market together in the evening, and yes one more thing was there but I forgot what it was)”, she explained her demands in place of my sorry.

“Theek hai, lekin abhi mujhko aaraam kaarne do, or wo jo tum bhul gayi thy wo sayad ye thy kya? (Ok,but for now, let me do some rest. And the thing which you forget was this only na?)”, I asked,giving her the chocolate which I brought earlier only.

“ Hann, yahi thi jo mein bhul gayi, thank you. Aacha chalo jao aab aur hair ,face wash kaar lo,pura raang laga hua hai (Yes, this is the only thing which I forgot, thank you. Now go and wash your hair and face,colors are spreaded there”,she said taking he chocos and leaving my way.

(I remembered someone made a quote years ago-“Kids and old people are the same”. Really they are, no doubt).

Chapter 4

The kids of my family and the neighbourhood were too much busy with themselves from the very early morning.

I was welcomed (by them) with the three small balloons (filled with liquid colors) attacks on me, which without any turn met their target and that is how patches of colours got printed on me.

"Happy Holi, Bhaiya",they said and ran away.

Their next target was the newspaper hawker. Those kids (who were in a ready position) were watching and waiting for him to come.

Very soon, the newspaper hawker came. Before he could reach to me (for giving the newspaper), he was attacked by them. He hadn't spoken anything but gave a smile looking towards them.

"Kids never leave anyone", I said (to him).

"Not of a problem. It is not the first attack on me, from the last of some year they came making me a target".

"And that's why you had covered all the newspaper with water proof plastic?"

"Yes, because If the papers will be ruined then it will be a great loss for me".

"It is fine. Happy Holi to you".

"A very Happy Holi from my side. Who did this attack on you in the very early morning?"

"The kids", I replied.

“Haappy Holi, Uncle G”, said the kids smiling and doing another attack on him from the front side.

“Happy Holi, cute kids, Enjoy”, said the newspaper and hurried with his bicycle before he was attacked anymore.

While reading the newspaper and walking inside my home, I was interacted by my father.

“Happy Holi, DaD”.

“Happy Holi, son .Go and meet your grandfather, he was asking about you”.

I agreed and went to meet my grandfather.

My grandfather (who was 97 years old) was just sitting in his wheel chair and having a cup of tea.

Whenever I come closer to my grandfather, my mind starts to memorize the happiest days of the very years ago.

[There was a time in the past when I and my elder brother went to have a daily evening walk in the nearby temple (surrounded by a park) with my grandfather. During that time, our grandfather shares a lot of things with us. He also asked a lot of questions from us. We enjoy a lot in giving the answers as in place of every correct answer we were offered with whatever things we wanted to eat from outside but not too much far from the radius of the temple. However, luckily there were almost a lot of shops in which a lot of things we like were available there. So there was no problem at all, many times we answered correctly but sometimes we both were failed too. Me and my brother had spent almost many years with the grandfather together than any other children in our family. Before two years, my grandfather’s leg stopped working and the hands slowed down the movement (as per the age) and because of that, we left going in the temple together. But we had almost spent many years going in the temple and still a lot of people nearby that area recognize us, the two grandsons with a grandfather).

“Abhijeet?”,he asked when I touched the feet of him.

(My grandfather’s memory power is also going weak day by day).

“Haan, dada g .Happy Holi (Yes, grandfather, Happy Holi)”.

“Happy Holi. Abhi bhi fever hai kya tumko? (Happy Holi. Are you still suffering from fever?)”.

“ Nahi ,dada g, aab sab kuch aacha hai (No, grandfather ,everything is fine with me now)”.

“Theek hai, lekinn jayada raang se maat khelna nahi toh fir se fever ho jayega (Okay, but don’t play much with colors or otherwise you’ll again suffer from fever)”,my grandfather warned.

“Theek hai, dada g. Aap bataiye aapko kaun raang laga diya hai (It is fine, grandfather. You tell me who had spreaded this colors on you)?”

“Aree woh water color nahi hai, powder color hai, choota baacha sab aakar laga diya hai (Oh that, that’s just a powder color, some small kids came and did this)”.

“ Sab bewkoof hai ,subah me humko aur paper wale koi bhi laga diya hai sab (They are all foolish, you know in the morning ,they attacked me and the newspaper hawker)”.

“Hahaha .... Koi nahi, jaane do. Tum bhi bachpan me to aise hi they (Hahah, no problem, leave them. You were also the same in your childhood)”.

“ Ho sakta hai magar fir bhi unlogo ne ye kuch jayada hi kaar diya hai (May be but still they have done something which is out of limit)”.

“Haan, wo toh hai. Aacha ,ek minute ruko, ek kaam hai tumse (Yeah, it is so. Wait for a minute, I have some work with you)”.

I remained sitting.

"Yeh lo aur jao Holi manao (Take this and go ,enjoy Holi)", grandfather said, giving me two paper notes of hundred.

"Thanks, dada g (Thanks, grand pa)".

"Theek hai, aab jao Abhijeet, masti karo (It's fine now Abhijeet go and enjoy yourself)".

*****

After meeting from my Grandfather, it was the time to participate in the Holi festival with the society friends who were about to come in half an hour (as per the previous planning).

Till then, I decided to get in touch with my girlfriend and friends to ask about what are they doing now? How are they celebrating this festival?

I switched on the phone. There were a lot of Holi blessings from my family, girlfriend and friends. I felt sorry for the reason that I couldn't switched to my phone in the very early of the morning. One by One, I tried to interact with all of them.

Anurag was there in between his long family (a joint family) and he was making some planning on how to enjoy this festival and make it a memory for future.

Some normal friends were engaged in the Virtual World of Social Media, some were travelling here and there and sadly some were packed in the square box of Hostel room. They were unable to come because of the Examination.

Anamika and her nearby friends were playing with spreading small small colours on each other's faces .Girls' can't go ahead of this but there's no doubt in saying that whatever they enjoy playing together (in their homes) is not less than us.

When I was still on the call with her, she told me something which was much more than a great surprise for me or it was something which I can't see in my dreams also.

She will be coming (not in my home, but in my colony) four houses far from my residence, three girls of different age live there ,in which one girl is the close friend of Anamika. She will be able to come because his father will also be coming as it was a good friendship and business partnership among Anamika' s Dad and her friend's Dad from the last fourteen years.

So, it was confirmed that she will be coming by 11: 30 A.M.

I was so much excited as I will be meeting her on this awesome day. Before I want to make a best plan, the door was knocked.

The colony friends came to take me out. My uncle (who unlocked the door) directed them to wait for ten minutes.

He told me that you can't go like this way. I hadn't understood. Few seconds later, I came to know that it was a danger planning. I decided to run but was unable in doing so.

My Aunty and my mother (who were making some foods in the kitchen) also came out from there. Three of them, made me so much colourful that I was unable to recognize myself.

"Now you can go", Uncle said to me.

When I came in front of my colony friends, they laughed seeing me.

"Oh, brother. He's already too much dipped in colours", they said, laughing.

"Yes, guys. You all are also not less dipped, something is remaining but don't worry I'll complete it in the way".

We went outside shouting and riding the bike like the most lafwoas (roadside romeos) do.

In the way, three crazy looking people were coming in the same manner as we were going, we were stopped by them who were none other than my brother's friends (who recognized me even if I was dipped in colours) and that's how I totally became mixed again in colours.

(The number of people you meet in Holi, the number of times colours gets added. These things continue till 1-2 P.M. of the day and after that those Dry Powder colours Holi comes into action).

There was too much colour on my whole body but still my colony friends hadn't stopped making me more colourful. I also exploited all of them.

After two hours spent between these colony friends, I went back to my home and washed myself to be recognized and identified by others and also to make sure that my girlfriend will not laugh at me seeing my condition.

When I became able to be identified, I walked across each and the every room but nobody was there except my Grandfather. All the family members were playing with the colours on the roof. As I had already played much more with colours, so I skipped going there. Playing with much more colours will be harmful for me.

So, I went towards the Grandfather's room (the way of the room was also from outside). There was a great gathering inside the room. In the festival days, his room becomes a public spot. Every relative and the society people come to meet my Grandfather in the festival days and because of that reason only, I was unable to meet with my own grandfather. If I will go inside the crowd then more and more people will meet me and after that one can understand what can happen on a day such as this!

I came out and went inside the kitchen to have some food.

Before I could be able to have a breakfast, Anamika informed me (through the phone call) that she's in my colony now.

I told her that I'll get it in touch within minutes and then after that I continued to concentrate on the same work which I was doing before the call.

(A short meeting with a girlfriend coming closer to home, is a bigger problem but whenever this happens, nobody wants to lose it, whatever plan we have to create, we will create it).

All my family members (who were on the roof) came downstairs. Without losing the chance, I ran towards the roof and called her (on the phone) to do the same.

As soon as she came on their roof without responding of my “Hi” through hand gestures, she started to throw the small balloons filled with colours (by which I was welcomed by the kids in the morning) on me. She was not alone at all, her stupid friend was also co-operating in this (looks like it was an earlier planning between them).

As it was a long distance Holi, so they had missed some shots but most of it attacked me directly. There was no option left with me rather than standing and being attacked by them. Suddenly, my eyes went on a small plastic bucket in which almost fifty of the balloons were in the ready to attack position. The developer and management of those items (the kids) were away from the radius. I took out all the balloons and started to throw them one by one to Anamika and her friend.

This game of throwing and attacking each other by using balloons went on for the next twenty minutes. The distance (between the two sides) was very far to talk but for throwing the water balloons, it was not so far. I called this kind of Holi- a long distance Holi.

Anamika was about to go downstairs, she called on my number.

I told her to meet me because after coming too much close with each other, it will not sound perfect if we don’t meet and also we had never met with each other since one and a half month, due to the exams.

We made a planning with each other through the phone call. I told her to come along with that friend in the Grandfather’s room (where more people from the society come so there will be no trouble and also the way of Grandfather’s room was from outside).

When both of them came inside the Grandfather’s room, some closer society boys, girls and some elders were also there. All those society people and Anamika ’s friend were known to my Aunty.

She told all the children ,Anamika and her friend to come inside the house for the reason of having a small lunch. My Aunty never allows any of our society children to leave without eating something from my home.

Though I was closer with Anamika but I couldn't talk to her, just because she was inside my home. If I will be talking to her then surely a special attention will be taken and may be a welcome to some of the troubles.

I was waiting outside silently for her and thinking that How fortunate am I that my own girlfriend is inside my home and she is being interacted with all my family members but with a different view, she's inside my home as our closest society relative, with whatever view she's there, I'm happy that finally she came inside my home and met my family.

The moment when she came out of the house, she said", Happy Holi and Bye" and walked with just a short notable greeting.

"Bye. Your shots were nice", I said to her.

(We both smiled looking at each other and remembering the far distance Holi we played together which had become the happiest memories).

Chapter 5

Our life was going very normal as there were no classes. These 2 months after the Class 10 are the only months where the student is free for long time and too much far from the classes and the boundaries of a campus. These two months are the first long freedom every student gets after around years of continuous education.

A raw hangout plan of our team was already in process, but a joint family festival ruined it at all. There was a first birthday celebration of a new-born kid in our family. This birth celebration festival of kid was in the attention of all the family members who are living in different-different parts of our country. Like each big family celebration unites all the family together like a Grand Re-Union, this event was also going to do the same.

I was given some duties and warned not to arrange any trips in between the days of the celebration. The celebration date was already postponed to 5 days more so that each family member from long distance can also come and join us.

Some family members living closer to our city were in the way of their journey and about to reach within a matter of hours.

The family decision makers were already busy with getting confirmed appointments of the Pundit G, the Event Hosting Tent Houses, Supporting Cooks and the Electric Lights designer who had done a lot of experiments but they were not even graduated also.

I was given the role of like a Tourist guy who has to pick up the family members from the Station and help them in reaching the

Hotel arranged for them. Some members were like the ones coming after years and years.

So they were explaining a lot while comparing the development of the Town from then to now. All of my friends were involved in getting re-union and I was somewhat settled between the old historical memories of my town, the memories were of such a long time when I was not born also.

Other than this, there was one more fact which was too boring stuff for me. Every of the far family members (coming after long time) were asking about the Education, Marks, Career and more related Questions.

Though we face lots of issues but a house full of family looks more than great and wonderful. This is the power of grand family union.

The next day morning

I was poked up by my siblings at such an hour which is like a mid-night for me. It was 5:00 A.M. and those kids were rounding me as if I am the culprit of a War. So finally, I had to wake up.

While coming from the roof to the Veranda, I noticed almost of all the members were sitting with a long discussion, and a cup of out-sourced tea from the chai-wala, who is bit closer to our house and that's why he offers some discount also.

When everyone noticed me, they started commenting and making fun of late wake-ups. Most of them were elders to me and they were comparing with their kids, who had to wake up at that hour just because of the Guardianship behind them.

I ignored the part with a half-smile and sat in the between them as the only option. All the seniors were having a debate about the

Movie Generation of their time to our time. Then the discussion moved forward to some random topics like Education these days and technology. And finally came the turn of Politics and then closure.

So, the next of three days were like that only and the fourth day was too much occupied regarding the Birthday which was on the 5th Day.

Once in a day time, I just got some minutes leave and switched to the phone. Being all covered with a lot of CCTVs like family members, I never had a single minute to talk with my Friends. A lot of random friends of school (who were also blank like us after the exam) had filled the Facebook and Whatsapp.

Inside those random messages, there was message from someone whose message was full of patience earlier and then of anger. I never notified her about the family event. Just to save myself from her calls in between the family, I added her number to the reject list, which she or anyone can understand because of the automatic cut-offs in each call.

It was my fault that I forgot to tell her. I tried to call her at that hour, but none of the calls were answered. I was like crossed in between the family, friendship and a relationship, the three things which are awesome part of Student Life. And sometimes, some of these attachments come to end when we create the barriers between them.

I kept calling her but the same thing happened.

After some packs of hours, I got a call from her. Though I was in between the throw backs of memories within the family but somehow skipped from there and picked up the call.

“Hello”, said a slow low voice.

“Hello Anamika. How are you? I am very sorry for not telling you the thing but please try to understand I was really busy because of the family festival”

“It’s okay”, she simply said without any extra crossings.

Her voice was telling she was not okay, and so I repeated it again.

“Are you okay?”

She was silent and the call was dropped.

When I called her back, the phone was switched off.

I was blank and hopeless for that moment. I wanted to reach out to her but, being helpless, I had to go back to manage the family function.

The Birthday Celebration Day

The day was very cool and the weather was also fine. Everything was fine, except Anamika. Her voice was still revolving in my mind which makes a lot of regrets to me. While everyone was glad and happy, I was like mixed of emotions. So, I decided and managed to call her just before some few hours of the beginning of the Birthday Party.

She picked up the call and also her voice was happy and fine. I asked her about the Yesterday’s responses.

“There was nothing wrong with me, my mobile phone was hanged”, she added.

"Oh. And what I thought was that you left me"

"Left me? But I am still alive"

"Not that left, here, it refers of leaving me behind"

"If this is so, then why you have added my number to the reject list?"

Somehow I consoled her and gave a beautiful turn to the conversation.

****

The birthday kid of 1 year old was excited but not so much. There were a lot of faces in front of her, in which only few of the faces were recognized by her.

In this technological era, everyone wants to have pictures and post it on Social Medias. And also a picture with a sweet kid makes the picture reach it to more and more people. So, everyone wanted to have a picture with the kid and that was a big trouble for the kid.

The event began with a cake cutting ceremony by such tiny hands which need one more hand to hold the plastic knife and cut the cake. During the beginning, they made her feel like a toy, that everyone can pick her up, take photos, pull the cheeks and then give it to the others one waiting. The other ones also do the same thing and the process continued.

The event went for a longer time, but it was a very happy memory with the members. From the very next day, all the far off members started to leave and go to their formal places. The house full of family was awesome but it again turned out to be empty.

CHAPTER 6

Animesh joined us.

The adventure trip began with a very in expensive happier turn as both of the drivers founded each other after seven years (who were best friends).

They both started doing the race with each other while driving and due to that, we reached the jungle ten minutes before.

(When we were about to go inside the jungle, the policeman stopped us at the gateway. We directed the drivers to fill the details in the guestbook (which is very compulsory to fill before going in the jungle). The drivers came outside, went together to complete the formalities of filling the guestbook).

After the guestbook was filled, the policeman said (to the drivers) : If there is rum with you, then give it to us, or otherwise if caught with it then three months jail and INR 25,000 penalty.

“Inspector Sahab, there’s no rum inside”, replied the drivers.

(Two policemen came and detected through the window).

“Ok, ok move”, they said (after detecting).

(The drivers came inside).

“Why are they inspecting the rum from us?”, Animesh asked.

“They were not inspecting you, they were inspecting us, the rum is banned here”, said the driver (while driving).

7 minutes later, we were in between the dense Udaipur jungle.

For the next five minutes, we keep on watching the forest cows whose group movement reminded us of 15th August parade in the old school.

We tried to go outside but the driver stopped us. He told that sometimes, these animals may attack us whenever they are in huge numbers, so it is not at all good to move outside (this time).

We came outside, after they had reached some distances.

One had to get registered on the next police sub- station, before moving inside the picnic spot and this time some security forces were also there along with the police men.

When the police men were doing our verification and registration, the security forces were introducing us with their warnings and restrictions.

Two of the security forces, walked together with us.

"Why there is so much restriction and security these days?",Avishek asked with the security guards.

"The crime is rapidly increasing here. The govt. sent us here for controlling the crime and giving safety to the visitors. Before coming here, we had 20 days of special training in which we had trained and told a lot about this area by our chief", he said.

"We were also directed by our chief to introduce every visitor with the rules and restrictions", said the other.

"Hmmm. I think we are safe from each and every corner", said Animesh.

"But if you will go near the restricted areas, then we will not be responsible of anything happening with you there", warned the security guard.

"Ok, I will not go there, but please remind me whenever you find me near the restricted areas, I may forget", Animesh quoted.

"Ok, ok, I am taking this responsibility of your", said the guard.

(We all moved ahead and reached to the picnic spot where the other members were waiting for us).

"Hi, Anamika g. This is me, Abhijeet from A-News. I would like to know your views about this area, so share your views about this jungle place", I asked to Anamika (doing the role of a journalist while making a video).

"Hi. Well, I think this area is awesome, a beautiful place for the nature lovers, a good scene. I can't tell more about this as I had just arrived few minutes before", she said.

"Ok, no problem. So how are you feeling right now (after coming here)?"

"Ummm, I am feeling free, happy and excited too".

"So Anamika g, what would you like to say about the forest animals here?".

"There are a lot of forest animals here, some are beautiful and some are dangerous. This forest area is dangerous and beautiful both".

"Yes, right. Now tell me how this place suitable for the love couples?"

"For them, it's a wonderful place, a romantic place".

"Thanks, Anamika g for giving your precious time for us. I hope you enjoy this area very much. Have fun, go ahead and enjoy".

"Thank you".

(The video recording stops).

"Abhijeet, it's my turn now".

"Of what?"

"I also want to do the same recording as you did".

"Sure, take it".

(Now, she started to create a video).

"Hello Abhijeet g, I am Anamika from Live News. I want to ask few questions from you (about this area).So are you ready for this?"

"Yes,ma'am".

"What is the best thing about this place? Share your views with us".

"This is an amazing place and I like it very much. The environment here is very fascinating, there is a very beautiful lake here, the dam is also very huge and wonderful and everything here is awesome and attracts a lot".

"When was the first time you came here?".

"I came here in summer of 2014 with for the very first time".

"So how was your first experience about this place?"

"My experience was same as you are feeling right now".

"Ok, Abhijeet. Thanks for your time. Enjoy".

"You're heartily welcome".(The video recording stops)

"Nice act, Anamika".

"Thanks , dear. Can we go near the lake side?"

"Yaa, off course".

We went towards the lake side where we meet all the friends. Everybody was sitting on the last stair (closer to the lake) and watching the beautiful scene from there.

Both the drivers were having some talks about their past memories of friendship.

We all boys went and sat on a locked ship and wished to have a boat ride. We tried finding some ways to do boating but unluckily no sailor man was available there.

We came out of there and asked the guards about the sailor men, they told that they are unaware about them.

When we were thinking on finding some other ways to enjoy boating, the drivers came near by us and the guards.

They asked (from the guards) : Do you have keys to unlock these boats?

"Yes, I have", replied the security guard.

"Then unlock it. We both have to do boating".

"Do you know how to sail the ships?"

"Ya..ya from the last seven years".

(The guard unlocked the boats).

We told the drivers that we also want to enjoy boating and that's how we all got settled on the boats, but before they start sailing, the girls noticed us, they came and sat on the boat without telling anything.

The guards told that the capacity of this boat is not more than seven persons.

I, Anurag , Animesh and the second driver had to come out of the boat.

We became sad.

"Don't worry. In the next trip we will go and they will watch", told the driver.

"But it was our idea to go for boating and now they are enjoying. We are watching sitting bored", Animesh said.

One of the security guard was very much happy about Animesh.

"Let's sort it out. We will go in another boat. I am unlocking it", he replied.

"You are also coming with us?"

"Yes, do you have any problem with us?"

"No, no, let us go together",Animesh replied.

(The guard unlocked the boat. We ran and sat there).

Both the security guards also came and sat among us.

“So from how many years are you doing the boating?”,Animesh asked (to the driver).

“I am a fresher and I don’t have much idea but I can do it somehow”, he replied.

“Really? Then sorry, I can wait for them to come, then I’ll go”, he replied.

“I was joking. It had been almost ten years of sailing. In my village area, there are many big rivers where I had enjoyed boating. It’s my past time”.

“Then, it is fine”, he said (sitting silently).

The driver cum sailor man started sailing the boat slowly.

Some minutes later, our boat was almost between the lakes.

The movement of that boat made us to feel so much uncomfortable that we felt the boat is going to sink, but it was not like that.

The guard told that there’s high speed water current in this big lake which, sometimes, disturbs the movement of the boat.

Without even much late, the driver sailed the boat away from the middle of the lake.

The boat became moving smoother now, without any disturbance.

Some minutes later, the driver became tired and told that he is unable to sail the boat much longer as it needs a lot of energy to sail the boat in a lake with high speed water current. He turned back the boat and sailed towards the corner of the lake.

“Boys, I am going to take a short rest. I’ll come back shortly “, he said after coming out of the boat.

"No problem", we said.

(He went towards the parking spot to rest inside the car).

We move ahead to get joined with the remaining friends who were waiting for us after they came from boating.

When we came closer (to them) then another driver asked: Where's he?

"He is resting inside the car".

"I am also tired a bit", he said and went towards the parking area.

We also thought of having a short break for lunch.

When we were having the lunch, Avishek and Neha disclosed a very great hidden news between us, they were also got tagged in a relationship with each other (from now).

Hearing this, we burst out of happiness when we came to know that Neha is the right one for Avishek. She was also a pretty and nice girl, however we don't have a very deep idea about her relationship but we can trust on her, she's a nice girl and intelligent and hard working too so there will be great pairing between both of them.

We also know that both of them will have no any extra idea on the matters which are not related with studies and all so they will be talking mostly on the matters related with studies or who knows if they both started loving each other truly then the matter will be different so it was not possible for us to predict that how their relationship will go, but we were happy that finally Avishek also got his girlfriend who is best for her and that's how this friendship group turned into a relationship group.

(As all the persons in the group are in relationship, so we thought of not giving much attention to friendship group as each members have the one to care for themselves and personally we thought that everybody will be busy in each other's relationship and care about his girlfriend/boyfriend only ,so the friendship group is no longer needed. But friendship group of the boys will be forever alive and the same five boys will be together as best friends).

*****

After having the lunch and knowing about that very great news, we decided to go inside the dense jungle to find some interesting animals and beautiful birds.

To our surprise, we found a lot of beautiful birds including different varieties of parrots and peacocks. Girls were too much excited (seeing the very beautiful and awesome creatures). A lot of people nearby us were taking photographs of these beautiful creatures. The beauty of that place (where these creatures are found in huge numbers) seems like a heaven and really it attracts a lot.

All of us friends and our girlfriend and the visitors had only one ambition with them and that was to touch those creatures but it was as difficult as an UPSC examination.

Our ambition remains incomplete, but suddenly we found one peacock shouting loudly in her melody. Everyone (who was nearby) got attracted towards her and started recording the video.

Few seconds later, the peacock opened her feather and then started enjoying in her own way. The scene was so much wonderful that there were no words for it.

Before we could take much video of the peacock, she noticed us and flied to some far distance. The peacock was gone, but the inexpensive scene was still in our eyes and in the video. We were feeling very lucky after this awesome moment.

We were planning to walk closer to that beautiful creature, but the weather hadn't co-operated us. We felt tiny droplets of rain from the sky which increased to heavy rainfall.

We ran towards the parking spot and went inside the car faster. The whole sky was full with black clouds which was symbolizing that this rain is unstoppable, so sitting inside the car and waiting for the heavy rain to stop was very boring at all. The drivers turned the car and started driving out of the jungle.

When Anamika reached to her destination and was about to left, she gave me a best hug.(She made the moment romantic but I still failed to kiss her due to someone's attention towards us and that's why we just had to end up this meeting with something not so special you can say).

CHAPTER 7

On the next day after that trip, we went to meet Animesh (who was very sad of his life). There was no great joy in him (like before). We tried knowing about the reason of sadness, but we got nothing.

When we asked him almost many times, then he said “She broke up”.

“Who?”,we asked.

“You don’t know her, I never told you guys about her and I think there is no need to tell you all now.

“Okay, as you wish”, Avishek said.

“So you are sad because she left you?”, asked Shreyansh.

He said, “Yes”.

“But what was the reason behind that break up?”, Anurag asked.

“ I don’t know ,everything was going fine, then suddenly before some days, she changed a lot (After leaving school),she started not to reply me and then after a week (after I came back from the adventure trip ending) she texted and broked all her connections with me”.

“Then I can understand what had happened, she’s interested in anybody else now”, Shreyansh said.

“May be”.

“This is the problem with most of the girls, they always want some new guy (periodically), they often break up when they find someone better than the present boyfriend”, Shreyansh said.

"Animesh, your problem is common, these days most of the guys are having same kind of problems associated with the break ups", Anurag said.

"Ya ,bro .That's right ,but I need her back. I love her very much".

"I can understand but sorry we can't do anything. Also she's not in Bettiah", Anurag said.

"Do you have some connections with any of her close friend? If yes, then try to find out the reason behind this break up through them. We can do something after the reason becomes clear to us", I said.

"No, I don't have".

"Then give us some days, we will try out finding some other ways".

(There was a great sorrow resembling on his face, he started losing interest in everything. From now, nobody can think he is (was) the happiest guy ever).

"Dude, I think this is the worst time for Animesh",Anurag said.

"One thing I hadn't thought (in my dreams also)that this thing will happen with Animesh and he will change like this way", I said.

"Yes, this break up is affecting him a lot and this time, he needs some support, so let us try making him happy".

"Ok, let us have some helpful conversations for him".

"Animesh, you are wasting your mood in thinking about her. Stop thinking, forget her. Wash off her name and everything, every time spent with her from your find, then you will feel relaxed", Anurag said.

"Do you think it is easy to forget the one who was everything for you? I'm not a girl that I will forget everything in a day and then on the next day will be found hanging out with other one", Animesh replied.

"That's right but by just remembering, you are not going to get her back in your life. This will affect you more and more (this time). That's why it is better to forget her",Shreyansh said.

"Then how to forget her?"

"Abhijeet, tell Animesh what had happened when Akshita left you", Avishek said.

"Yes, that may be helpful", Shreyansh said.

"But before that, Shreyansh and Anurag, tell Animesh about how both of you dealt with the situation when both of your girlfriends were separated for a long decade".

"When Nandini went far from me, I missed her a lot but there was a belief and a deep faith that one day I will meet her and propose her which I hadn't done when we were studying in the same class. Luckily, after some years I founded her on social media, proposed her there and now we are together as you see us today. As I met with Nandini after years so you will also meet her one day. Don't lose faith", Anurag said.

"Some things are not in our hand and what we can do is "Waiting ",if you can wait then you can get her back too. Only those can wait whose love is true and true love never dies. ", Shreyansh said.

"Very true lines, wonderful Shreyansh", I said.

"Thanks, now tell Animesh how you felt when Akshita left you", Shreyansh said.

"Though I loved Akshita truly, but she was not at all real to me, she had told hundreds of big lies to me and we never had some best memories. I never tried getting her back with the whole of my heart but I was disturbed for some days feeling and thinking about her. When she leaved me, I got to know a lot of bad things about her which totally made me go away from her and after that I thought –Everything happens is good. Had she not been broke up with me then I never get to know so much things about her and still I will be living with the same fake girlfriend".

"But you loved her truly?"

" But it is not at all necessary that the girl you loved truly is real to you, and what is the need to be in relationship with a girl who lied so much, she may have some more big lies. We only know the things which are disclosed to us but still there are many things we don't know. Then at this moment, it is totally fair not to try to get her either it was your true love", Shreyansh said.

"Animesh, I suggest you to learn how to live alone, to survive with this ups and downs of your life because in everyone's life there's comes a point when the loved ones leaves or forgets (like your girlfriend) and that situation affects both the mind and the heart. Once you will learn how to leave alone then there will be no much effect on you and your career if someone leaves you",Avishek said.

"But if you will remember and miss her all the time then it will do a great harm to you and your life. You will not achieve anything, your career will get ruined, and nobody will give you a value if you will not achieve anything.

Your family members will also not support you if you hadn't achieved anything. The world will make fun of you. If a girl will not do anything, then there will be no problem at all as there will another one to feed and care her but if a boy will not do anything then it will be a disaster for him. So if you want to do something for yourself, then wake up, forget her and stay on a single track", Anurag said.

"But how to do this, guys? I am completely unable to forget her".

"If you will not remember her, then shortly you will forget her. There are a lot of things to do in life, a lot of things to know, to understand and to learn. You can engage your mind in anything you like the most",Avishek said.

“You are right. I will focus on something useful and also I’ll try not to remember her”.

“Good. I wish you forget her soon”, Avishek said.

Animesh nodded.

“Ok guys, now listen here. I am going to Kolkata for a 20 day trip excluding the travel time”, I said.

“So when are you leaving from Bettiah?”, Anurag asked.

“I will go after days”.

“Where you will stay in Kolkata?”, Avishek asked.

“To Akriti’s home”.

“Bro, I will also go to Kolkata but my trip is after a week”, Shreyansh said.

“Really? So where will you be staying?”

“To my Aunty’s home, she’s staying in Chandan Nagar”.

“Wow, then we will meet and enjoy there”.

“Sure, just wait for a week”.

“But Abhijeet ,I am not understanding one thing: How can you stay to Akriti’s home?”,Animesh asked.

“There is a good turn between Akriti’s family and my family. Both of our sisters had studied engineering and they were together for more than five years”, I said.

“Do they know that you are coming?”, Avishek asked.

“Yes, off course. This plan was been discussed among us from a month”.

“Where does she stays in Kolkata?”, Anurag asked.

“Sealdah, near about 1 kilo meter from the main Kolkata city”.

"I will be living almost forty kilo meters from the main city", Shreyansh said.

"Yes, dude but forty kilo meter is not so far. It will just take an hour hardly to reach Kolkata city", I said.

"Yes right. We'll make a plan together to visit some famous places after a week", Shreyansh said.

The phone rings before I could say something to Shreyansh. It was a call from my Mom, I picked up the call.

She told that there is some urgent work at home and ordered me to come home soon.

I said "bye" to my friends and hurried towards my home.

CHAPTER 8

10:00 AM

FRIDAY

When I entered inside the train, I saw two persons sitting on the place which was reserved for me. I told them that It's my reserved seat but they reacted as if they had not listened what I said. I told them the next time but still they hadn't responded.

After few minutes, the TTE came inside the train and started checking the ticket of the passengers. When he came closer to them and asked about the ticket, one of them fetched out a single person ticket (which was a waiting ticket) and showed to the TTE.

While checking the ticket, the TTE asked ",Is the person unavailable?"

"No, I'm here only", I said.

"Then why not you are seating at your place?", he asked.

"They were not moving", I replied.

The railway policeman (who was together with the TTE) came near them and ordered to leave the seat.

Both of them stood up and were about to go but unluckily the TTE stopped them.

"You both are together but you showed me only a single adult ticket. Where is your ticket?", asked the TTE from the second person (in an angry mood).

He remained standing like a statue.

The TTE understood and started preparing his ticket along with the fine charge.

"Where are you travelling to?", he asked (from him) while making a penalty ticket.

"Durgapur", he said.

The TTE forwarded him the ticket and asked for money. The total cost was Rs.1400. He had no any other, so he had to pay extra charge to take the penalty ticket.

After both the persons left, I finally sat on my place.

The TTE looked at his reservation chart and called my name.

"Yes", I said.

"Show me your ticket and the proof of identity".

I kept out my Aadhar card along with the ticket and gave him.

After checking he returned me the ticket and the Aadhar card. He also warned me not to allow any person to sit on my place.

After the TTE left, both the persons came and requested (from me) to shift some distance (so that they'll be able to sit) telling that: Everyone has to manage during travelling.

I replied, "I had to stand ten minutes just because of you both. If you can't manage without ticket then why will I manage if I already have the ticket and my seat is also confirmed".

They became unable to speak something and silently walked to some other places. From the last half an hour, I was looking out from the window of that moving train. When I became bored, I went to the upper birth and to have a short sleep as I have to awake the whole night during this journey.

*****

7:30 PM

The railway waiter came and woke up me for asking the order of tonight's dinner.

"When would you like to have your dinner?", he asked me after noting down my orders.

"Bring it as soon as it's ready", I said", but before that bring a bottle of cold water".

When he went to bring the water, I switched to my mobile phone and texted

Anamika : Hi......my princess. What's going on there? ?

Three minutes later, she replied.

Anamika : Hello, I'm just watching the television. Where are you now? Are you enjoying your journey?

Me: No not at all, I'm getting bored here.

Anamika: May I know the reason why are you feeling bored?

Me: Yes, sitting in a train during a long journey makes me feel bored ?.

Anamika: Then, I am not going to sleep tonight.

Me: Why?

Anamika: I can't make you feel alone. We will chat together till the whole night.

Me: Thanks for that but you don't have to do this.

Anamika: Why not?

Me: Because I don't want you to do this, so don't destroy your sleep for me.

Anamika: But you can't ruin my plan. I had slept all the day just to wake up at night because I knew that you will be feeling lonely and bored there.

Me: That's right, my princess. Thanks for doing this for me.

Anamika: Welcome, my prince. This will be the longest conversation between us ever.

Me: Excuse me, Ma'am. Can we have 15 minutes of break for having the dinner?

Anamika: Ya, sure Sir, tell me when are you going to have your dinner?

Me: I'll tell you when the railway waiter will come back with the food.

Anamika: Ok, fine. So how much journey is left from now? How many times it'll take to reach the destination?

Me: It will take near about 6-8 hours more. May I ask a personal thing from you?

Anamika: Ok, ask.

Me: How much sacrifice can you do for your love?

Anamika: I can't tell you this but let me make you clear that I'm not going to leave you at any cost in future and also I'm ready to cross every hard time but I'll never ever leave you.

Me: Can you fight with your family for your true love?

Anamika: Somebody said that, "When you are true then there's no need to fight for justice, but if you are false then you are not eligible to fight for it". Based on this, once the right time will come, I'll request my parents for this, more over I'll be trying to do whatever I can do but I'll never make my parents feel ashamed of me and also I'll never leave my true love.

Me: Wow, great. I liked your answers.

Anamika: And what will you answer if I'll ask the same question with you?

Me: I want to reach such a height that once I'll reach there then every father will happily give the hands of her daughter to me. My family will also set me free to do anything as per my wish except doing the illegal things.

Anamika: So you want me or any other daughter?

Me: Honestly, I only need you. I had done a commitment with myself that in order to get my true love I'll fight for everything, I'll fight with my failures and the problems coming in my life, however I will not make sure that I will be successful or not , but where ever I'll be, I'll not be so much smaller that I can't deserve my true love. This is my commitment for my true love.

Anamika: Great, so this is reason why you that you always remain free and satisfied?

Me: Yes, everybody can achieve whatever they want to achieve, there must be a complete desire and the potential to fight with the problems.

Anamika: Yes, you're right. I hope and wish that you'll complete the commitment you made with yourself.

Me: Thanks. Dear, my phone is not charged so I'll be able to chat after half an hour, till then go and do your dinner, please.

Anamika: But where will you charge the phone? Is the facility available there?

Me: Yes, the small power plug is just closer to my seat.

Anamika: It's fine then. Bye, charge your phone. I'll text you after thirty minutes.

Me: Okay. Bye

I texted her, kept my mobile phone in charge and went to the Pantry Car and ask about my order.

When the railway waiter saw me, he told that in five minutes he will be back with the food. I told him that you forgot to give a bottle of cold water. He apologized and gave me the water.

I went back to my seat.

*****

Half an hour later ....

After completing my dinner, I switched on my phone. It was only 53% charged, so I resumed using it while charging only.

As soon as I switched on the phone, a message arrived from her.

Anamika: Hi, once again. Had you completed your dinner?

Me: Yes, tell me how are you feeling now? Are you sleepy?

Anamika: No, I'm not. Are you?

Me: No, so are we really going to talk the whole of this night?

Anamika: Yes, yes. Do you have problems with this?

Me: But you will get bored in continuously talking with me.

Anamika: No, but I think you are getting bored in talking with me.

Me: No dear, I'm not.

Anamika : Ok ,so tell me where have you decided to take admission in Class 12th?

Me: I haven't decided anything regarding this, yet.

Anamika: Where will you stay? Will you live in Bettiah or at some other place?

Me: I'm not going to live in Bettiah at any cost. What about you?

Anamika: I am also not going to live here, but wherever we will go, I will be closer with you through the heart.

Me: What if you got a handsome person there?

Anamika: Stop doing talks of this stupid kind.

Me: I like the moment when you get fired with me.

Anamika: Ok, so here it is What if got a beautiful and gorgeous girl there and your heart started to beat 10 times faster seeing her, then what will you do?

Me: Hahaha. I never look at the face of any girl except you and also it is nearly impossible for me to get patch with any other girl, no matter how much beautiful she is! My heart only beats for myself and my life: that's you.

....................the talk continued..................

For the next five hours, we continuously talked on a lot of issues which we had never talked. We discussed a lot of things together and also made a lot of plans and promises with each other.

We came to know each and everything about each other (through that conversation) from family to career and the future goals. We also shared some very personal problems of our life which we have never shared with anyone, not any friend and family member. Also, we came much closer than before after knowing each and every reality of our life.

*****

4:00 A.M.

SATURDAY MORNING

Chakarborty Uncle (Akriti's father: A senior civil engineer of a construction company) was coming to pick me at Howrah Junction.

(I and Akriti treat each other as best friends forever but her family members treat both of us like brothers and sisters and this is the reason why I never plan my trip to West Bengal in the month of August).

He called on my phone (to know the exact location of the train).

"Namastey Uncle",I said (after picking up the call).

"Namastey Babu. Where's the train now?"

"In twenty minutes it will be reaching at Howrah Junction".

"Ok,I'm also coming in fifteen minutes. There will be a lot of crowd at the junction , so you will come directly near the exit gate. I will be there".

"Ok, uncle",I said.

From Asansol, a lot of local people had crowded the train. When I told them to give me some space as I was going to keep my bags down which I had kept on the upper birth, they said something in Bengali which I hadn't understood and remained silent.

Two minutes later, the train stopped at an unknown station. A man who was looking like a literate person came inside and sat between us.

I tried to communicate with him to ask help in keeping my bags down but I don't know in which language I'll communicate with him. Finally (with a bit of fear),I told him (in English) to help me in keeping my bags down, fortunately he responded and helped me in doing so ,also he managed some space and kept my bags there. I thanked him for whatever he did for me.

(Before meeting with that person, I was feeling like being ignored as nobody was able understand my language, they only speak Bengali, however some Hindi speakers are also there but with a Bengali tune. Sometimes, when they speak something in Bengali, it sounds just like they are abusing).

When the train reached at Howrah Junction, I picked the luggage and came out from the train.

After twenty meters walk, I saw Chakarborty Uncle and walked closer to him.

A taxi driver was also standing along with him, who picked up my luggage and went out of the station (to the taxi stand). I and Chakarborty Uncle were also coming out of the station walking slowly with having some conversation.

Forty-five minutes later, the taxi reached Akriti's home.

Rachna Aunty (Akriti's mother) and Shreejata Di (Akriti's elder sister and my sister's friend) were fine awake but Akriti was still in her dreams.

I was having some general conversations (what people talk if they meet after years) with Aunty and Shreejata Di.

"You still look the same as you were some fine years before",Shreejata Di said (pulling my cheeks).

"Yes, may be".

"So how was your journey?"

"You must be tired, na?",Aunty asked.

"I wasn't tired in the train but I'm tired now (after travelling by a closed taxi)".

"Then Abhijeet, go and do some rest. You will feel better".

"No, Aunty, it's all fine. I am not too much tired to go to rest".

"Ok, Abhijeet then I'm going in the near Durga Temple, If anything will be needed then ask from Shreejata Di".

"Okay, Aunty".

"Does Aunty daily visit the Durga temple?"

"Yes, she's late today. She woke up very early in the morning to go and worship in the temple".

"Oh, nice".

"How is your hometown Bettiah?"

"It is developing very fastly".

" Aacha, how many new things are there?"

"I can't describe but know that everything is changed from then to now".

"Then it is the need to go and visit there".

"Yes, why not? You're welcome. When are you coming to Bettiah?"

"I don't know when but shortly I'll be coming. The visit to far off places became a dream for me from the moment when I got the job. Hardly, I get any long term holiday".

"The same problem is with my sister also".

"Yes, she also keeps mentioning it whenever I ask her meet me here".

"Hmm, don't you both get the holidays at the same time?"

"Two years before, we have got that and then we went on a trip to Kasauli".

"Wow, nice. Is Akriti still sleeping?"

"No but let us go and make her awake".

"Ok".

“Hey Akriti, wake up”, said her sister.

(No any response)

“Wake up, how much you will sleep?”,said she, again.

“Don’t disturb me”,she replied in half sleepy mood.

“Why?”,I asked.

“Who is this?”, she asked from her sister without opening the eyes.

“Do you forget that Abhijeet is coming this morning?”

“It’s me, stupid”,I said.

She woke up in a shock.

“Hey, Abhijeet, hii. Good morning. I was just out, that’s why, I woke up lately but trust me, I had a planning to wake up before your arrival”.

“No problem, Akriti. Good morning”.

“Thanks. So how are feeling here?”

“I’m fine but I think you are still in the half sleep, so bye and have a half sleep”, I said to her.

“No, no, I am not in sleep”, she replied, coming out”.

“Now you are”.

“Abhijeet, I am going to make a tea”, her sister said and went in the kitchen.

“Had you slept the last night during journey?”

“No, I was awake”.

“You know, last night I hadn’t slept since 2 A.M.?

“What were you doing till 2 A.M.?”

“I was so much excited, that I kept making some plans”.

“Hmmm, but when I came here, you were travelling in the dreams”.

“Yes, but what problem? I’m awake now”.

(Her sister came back with the tea).

“So any new planning discussion for today?”, Shreejata Di asked.

“Not for today, sister I want to have a sleep”.

“So my today’s planning is going to be wasted by your sleep?”,Akriti quoted.

“Honestly, yes. But we will use that plan for tomorrow”.

“Thanks for that, but, I’ve some other plans for tomorrow”.

“Alright, as you wish”.

“But you will have to do one work for me”.

“Which work? Please elaborate it”.

“I had been telling my friends about you. You will be meeting time this evening and I don’t want to listen ‘no’ for an answer of it”.

“If it is so, then I’ll meet them, ok now?”

“Ya, much better”.

“Then bye for now. I’m going to sleep”.

“When will you wake up?”

“Near about 1:00 P.M. -2:00 P.M.”

“Wait for some minutes, the food will be ready soon”, Shreejata Di said.

“Thanks, sister but I can’t eat now. I’ll have the food after I will end with a good sleep”.

"Ok, no problem, but don't be shameful in asking anything, you were too shameful in your childhood".

"But now, I'm not".

"Great then, a very happy good night"

1:40 P.M.

When I woke up, Aunty told me to have a food first. I was already afraid of the food problems I had to deal in West Bengal.

When I tasted the food, I became surprised.

"Who made this?", I asked from Akriti.

"Shreejata Di".

"What happened? Is it bad?", Shreejata Di asked.

"No, no, It is not bad. Just I'm surprised to have it here. There is not a slight difference in this food from what I eat in my region".

"It's thanks to your sister. She made me learn and trained me to cook North Indian foods".

"You have well practiced How to make it, I liked it".

"Thanks, but I don't know making more recipes".

"Then do one thing. There's an application which can make you able to cook whatever you want".

"What's the name of that application?"

"Big oven. Download it from the Google Play Store".

"Don't talk and eat fast, friends will shortly be coming".

"I can't. Let them come".

“See the app, it’s the same only na?”,Shreejata Di asked while showing the mobile phone.

“Yes, it is”.

(Akriti’s friends came inside. She went out, reminding me to join soon with them).

In order to meet the Bengali friends, I came outside. There were two boys and three girls: Satchit ,Chirag, Paloma, Rujula and Adaya.

Adaya and Rujula were asking more things from me which I was replying somehow because half of their words were floating out of my mind as they were using the Bengali ascent in speaking.

Before they could say something more, Satchit and Chirag came and began to talk with me. Both of them were speaking slowly and not with much Bengali ascent so it was a bit easy to understand them.

After I spent some time talking with them, I became able to recognize their voice and soon became able to talk with everyone and giving the right reply to their words but still the language problems made me uncomfortable because sometimes when these friends talk with each other in Bengali, I became unable to understand and it seems something bad to me but It was not like that in reality they were friendly and co-operative.

We all planned to visit the awesome place Science City on the next of the day which is almost 5 kilometers far from Sealdah if we go through D.C. Dey Road and then on every day we planned to visit different places. We enjoyed together so much and much more than them I enjoyed visiting to the different famous places together with them.

The last sixteen days spent in West Bengal became a best memory. We had visited Water Park, Nicco Park, Indian Museum including Indian Botanical Garden and many more places.

CHAPTER 9

After six days from my arrival to Bettiah, I and Anamika planned to meet(after so many days) at the Park Restaurant (based on the name, this restaurant was like the park with some beautiful flowers, plants and trees situated near-by.

We planned to go there at 5:00 P.M. (in the eve).

For such a great occasion, that we are going to meet together after more than a month, we both were very happy and wanted the time to move fast.

At 4:45 PM, I became ready came out from my home to reach the Park Restaurant (which was a kilo meter far more my home and 2.5 kilo meter far from Anamika's home).

Anamika called on my number. She was riding her sister's scooty and will be reaching in ten minutes, so I also thought of taking my brother's bike. I came back to my home and asked the keys from my brother.

Five minutes away, I reached the city park and called her. She told me to stay there only telling that she will be coming in just a couple of minutes.

I switched off the engine and started to play Candy Crush.

Suddenly, a girl on a scooty came to my side and stopped there. Her both hands and face was covered with the protective clothes which saves their skin from being damaged and rough in the hot sun (Girls are very much cautious about the protection of their skin and face as girls are girls. We (boys) don't even care much on this).

For the last few seconds, she was continuously looking at me but she didn't said anything to me. I was also silently gazing at her. I knew that It was Anamika but to be confirmed, I quitted the Candy Crush and gave a call on her phone. She, then, kept her phone inside the pocket. I became confirmed that it's Anamika only.

"Why were you not speaking?", I asked when I went closer to her.

'Because you were failed to recognize me"

"But how can I recognize you? You were all covered except the eyes".

"But you may have spoken my name".

"Like an idiot? What if there was some another girl in place of you, then?"

"Then........"

"Then, what?"

"I don't know. Leave it".

"Ok, let us go to the Restaurant now".

(Park restaurant was almost 500-600 meter away. We were riding together with the same speed).

At the Park Restaurant

"May I have a clean photograph of your eyes? Next time it'll help me in recognizing you ".

She took out all her protective clothes (or whatever name it is, I don't know) and quoted (smiling)", Is it okay now?"

"Yeah, much better",I replied.

We sat on round table no.3 which was closer to some beautiful flower plants.

I plucked one of the flowers and offered it to her.

"It's not your thing, what you gave me but thank you".

"Alright then here it is", I said and presented her the five beautiful flowers wrapped together (which I bought from a Nursery which was closer to my home).

"Wow, awesome, wonderful", she acted while touching those flowers, "From where you have got this?"

"From the nature".

"I asked about the place".

"Nature is also a place".

"Do you like nature?"

"Yes, very much. You?"

"Yup, I am also fascinated and fond of this nature and it's beauty but rarely the nature will attract us anymore, the pollution and deforestation is destroying the very beauty of the environment and the nature itself".

"That's right, we all are self-responsible for this".

"Yeah but the Non-Government Organizations (NGO's) and many other Nature Conservation Organizations are discovering some ideas and plans to save this awesome nature".

"It is true but, let's not discuss about this issues now. We can focus on these issues later (at home)".

"Oh, sorry".

"Ok, no need to apologize. Would you like to have some non-vegetarian foods?"

"Noo, I don't want to eat non-veg this time. How about a vegetarian lunch?"

"Yes, tell me what to order?"

"Dosa, Samosas and Chaat".

"Only?"

"Yes, do you want something else?"

"Do you like sweets?"

"Sweets like?"

"The gulab jamuns and the Creamies".

"Before this, you never asked about having some sweets, but, now after coming from Kolkata why are you asking this? I think you became likely to this after eating the sweets made by the hand of Bengali sweet makers".

"Yes, exactly the same happened. The Bengali sweet makers are the toppers in sweet making. The sweets were the only thing which suited me and I liked it. Rest, all the food stuffs were completely different from us. Mostly, I survived on sweets, cakes or the Home made Northern foods in Akriti's home".

"Does Akriti's mother have the idea about North India food?"

"No as she never travelled to North India in her life. It was her sister who knows about it. She had lived in North India so she has complete idea and also she makes wonderful North Indian foods".

"Ohh, great, so it was no any trouble there regarding the food problems".

"Yes, thanks to her sister. Let us order the foods now".

The waitress was called, we told him about the things we decided to eat.

She noted the orders and walked away in silence.

"Your dress is very beautiful. I like it's colours and design both. It's much closer to what Taylor wore in the Love Story"

"Thanks, there. If you don't mind may I ask why you often wear the clothes and comb your hair like the professionals?"

"It's my normal hairstyle as my hair moves in one direction only. I will have to spend an hour If I want to change my hairstyle which I never spent and about my cloth wearing, I don't like any other styles and also I feel comfortable with my present style. I don't focus much on this that how am I looking. I only want my comfort".

"But you look very much awesome with your present style. It suits you very much than any other person. I like this, don't try to change it in future".

"I don't know if you are making fun of me or anything else, but thank you for whatever you said".

"I'm not making fun of you. It's true".

(The waitress came and kept two plates dosas on the table).

"Ok, thanks for that. let's eat this Dosa now".

(The Dosa was too much chilly and spicy that we couldn't eat more than half of it as both of us can't tolerate much chilly and spicy foods).

Anamika called the waitress and asked for water and also requested her to tell the Chefs not to add much chilly powders and spices on the Chaat. She understood and did the same within a minute, the Chaat was there on the table.

(The waitress who saw us feeling more uncomfortable was worried about us. We told her that ,it was not the fault of them. We hate spicy and chilly foods and we had ignored these from many years. Mostly, we are fond of the foods with general spices).

After drinking almost two –three glasses of water, we came in our moderate zone.

Then we tried the "Chaat".It was tasty and not spicy at all so none of the trouble was in eating it. In fact, it was very tasty and we enjoyed it.

The waitress came and asked, "How was that?"

"Excellent".

"Superb",Anamika added.

"Thanks, Ma'am and I'm sorry to say that there's no Samosa in our stock (which you have ordered)",she apologized.

"No problem, bring the Gulab Jamuns and the creamies then", she said to her.

Anamika got a call from his home. She received it and after a minute of talk, she said(to me)standing up, "I need to go now. My elder sister told that Dad will be coming in between thirty-forty minutes. I need to go before that time or otherwise I will be scolded badly".

(The waitress was back with the sweets).

"Just sit down, calmly. Thirty minutes is a very huge time. You can reach your home in just twenty minutes from now".

"Yeah but what if it took much more time than that? If I had got blocked in between the traffic, then?

"You will not. If you want me to be alone, then you can go or silently sit here for the next five minutes".

She sat down without speaking anything.

In the next of the five minutes, I requested her to join me on eating the sweets which was already ordered for her. I also made her believed that she will definitely reach her home before the arrival of his father. She became relaxed then.

As soon as we finished, she stood up and took out a book from her hand and told me: It's the slam book which I forgot to give you for filling it at the earlier stage of our relationship. The next page after "Me" is blanked, you will have to fill it there only.

"Okay, no problem, I'll fill it. Bye, my sweet heart".

"Bye", she said and moved ahead.

Few seconds past, she came back and quoted "I forgot something".

"What?", I questioned.

She hadn't told anything, she just came silently and kissed me on the lips for more than ten seconds.

"This", she replied and walked towards the scooter.

After Anamika left, I came back to the table, paid the bill and continued to leave.

The waitress called me, "You forgot something".

"What?", I was confused.

(When this word came out from my mouth, I recalled that the word was recently used by me, but the purpose was different).

"This", said the waitress showing the book given by Anamika).

I ran to take the book and also thanked her for notifying me. If it had been a single minute late, then I will be too much away from getting it.

At the Home

As soon as I reached to my home, I texted Anamika: Had you reached your home? What about your Dad?

Anamika: Yes, my Dad will be coming after 15 minutes.

Me: I knew that, but you were very worried and also in a hurry.

Anamika: Oh, I'm sorry for that. Where are you ,now?

Me: I'm also at my home. Bye, we will talk in the mornings".

Anamika: Good night, sweet dreams, my prince. Love you, bye.

Me: Same to you, princess. Good night.

I went to my room and opened her slam book (to fill up) but as soon as I had opened it, I found that she had mistaken (as she was in hurry) her slam book with the colourful diary (whose cover page was also looking like a SLAM BOOK).May be, both of them were of the same size or same colour.

I kept her diary safely and planned of reading it on the other day.

Next morning, I switched to her diary and saw that all the good and bad happenings of her own life were mentioned there.

When I turned some pages around, I noticed that there was a symbol marked on the above of a page.

All the pages (from there) were mostly related with her life at school, about her boyfriend, the friends circle, her family and more.

As every curious boyfriend, I also focused on to know that- what she really feels about the boyfriend (about me)? And every of the things related with me. I ignored all the entries.

Entry 29

Our group "Happy Buddies was going to be closed after Animesh left Bettiah and went to Haridawar and few more reasons were also behind that.

We ,girls, don"t wanted this to be happened as the group had taken a major place in our life. We opposed this as something good was attached with that group which we don"t wanted to lose.

Also if the group will be finished, then I"ll be unable to meet the guy (who became a special part of me from the previous four months).

I am in love with Abhijeet ,but I don't know how to tell him about my feelings and about my love for him.

Though he is silent and cool but these days he is very serious and broken now. I don't know how to tell him about this (right now) but I don't want to lose him.

In the evening, I will try telling Anurag and ask about this Group problem.

(I turned the page and landed on the next entry).

Entry 30

The group was saved from being closed. We were together again but this time with some of the promises made for each other and also reforming in an awesome way.

There was still a problem troubling me: I had yet not decided ⍰ how to speak about my true love in front of him.

I was much closer to Abhijeet (than any other girl in the group) but still I am not successful in telling him about my heart.

Today morning, I think he was angry with me as he had not replied any of messages (which never ever happened before). I was worried and disturbed about this.

When I called Anurag, he told me each and everything: He was not angry with me, but he was completely heart broke thinking about the broke up of a finished connection (which reminds her or whatever name she has).It"s her birthday today. I don't know why most of the boys always stick to the memories of that girl whose existence in their life was the past.

After getting it known by Anurag about the real problem, I thought this is not the right time to tell him about these all things of myself.

But when will the right time come?

I'm finding the answer of this question only.

Entry 31

Today, I found myself too much far from him. The so closer I wanted to go in his life, I went very much far from him and his life.

My close class friends told me to kill my feelings for him and were referring me to forget about him. They told me to accept the proposal of Shenoy (who had proposed me almost seven – eight times). I never listened to them and because of that there came a barrier between me and the close friends.

I was a born stubborn in wanting or getting the things happen according to my choice.

Once my mind came on anything, I never skipped getting out of the way or in the middle of the way. I always try to get it at whatever cost.

Leaving my true love was not the one which I wanted to do.

I only tried to focus on : What the problem was which made me too far from him?

The trouble was, it was with me only.

It was a lack of understanding with me. The thing which I did was, blindly loving him only.

I was just waiting for a perfect time, how boring?

He or nobody will believe me at one time when I'll go directly (or indirectly) tell him about my true love.

From today, I will be improving all the problems, which is like an obstacle in my love story: That is my commitment with myself.

Entry 32

I'm feeling bored, very much bored and upset of my life as something unusual came to happen with me (one by one) from the very first day when I grew younger and became self-sufficient to realize everything.

I asked for help from my sister. She asked: What is it which is troubling you now?

I shared my first love (with her) and the problems related with it.

She got my point and understood my problems.

She asked directly: What is Love?

"Love is life and life is love", I answered.

She marked it.

"Love is such a thing that without it we and the world is no thing".

She told me my faults and also she pointed out the way in which I was going on to get my true love. It was totally wrong.

I asked her from where she had got that much idea on this. She said nothing but her smiled told everything.

I understood it. Some secrets came out.

From that time, we both were sharing the things related with each other love and also tried sorting out the problems together.

Entry 33

The next week was very wonderful for me. I became successful in showing him every sign and symbol to tell him that I Love Him the most (I was not able to tell him, directly). I also began to give him much respect than I had given to any other boy.

For the very first time, I felt something good in my life (after years) , the way he talked with me was a kind of memory for me and will be a memory for any girl.

I told him each and everything whatever good or bad happened in my life. When he also started to share some of the good and worse times happened in his past life, I felt very free and unlocked all the major problems troubling me in my life (which I had not told anybody, not my sister also). It was all cleared and I was feeling well and lighter.

I was fortunate with myself for the days from the beginning of the next week.

There was also a great surprise I came hearing that week. We were going to meet in the year end party of the group which will held on

I have decided that on 8th March, I will tell him what was in my heart.

Now I am trying to make a fixed time on how to tell him. I did everything which a true lover does, but telling him directly is also important.

Thanks God, for this week. I love my life because my life loves me.

When I finished reading that entry, I was not with myself. I got stuck with the same moment and my feelings. I was also thankful to God for that week. She kept all the things away which were going rough in my life.

I never thought that one day I will be meeting such a nice girl as the true love. She had the solution to my every problem and mostly she always understood my views in a right direction. She made me enjoy my life again (which was a history of months and months before).

It was like a magic happening not only for her but for me also.

I continued to read.

Entry 34

Happy Buddies party-day

There was a very happy moment in the whole group. As soon as all the friends of our group met together, we were sharing some of the funniest and best memories spent with Animesh.

Abhijeet (who was sitting beside me) came to notice me personally which he never did.

After the whole awesome moments spent on the phone calls and the Mobile SMS, it was our first interaction when we felt each other not as a friend but something more than that.

We felt something for each other what we call it: sharing, caring, understanding, realizing in background level and LoVE in the front level.

Abhijeet began his talk with a funny critical comment on me. Before something good was about to start between us, Shreyansh and Anurag invaded this goodness among us. They were curious to tell what better they came to know just at the moment. Anurag found her lost love (fortunately) on Facebook.

Shreyansh also got this patch up (again) with the same girl.

Both of them continued to share about these things happened with them in brief. Due to their this happenings, a barrier came in between me and Him but I became unable to stop them as it was also a great pleasure for them, that they got their true love back. This pleasure was also not small in front of my happiness.

But the moment when they were going too far with their discussion on their love story, I had to come in between of this.

Indirectly, I told Abhijeet what was left for me to say (for which I was waiting for a perfect time) and proposed him.

The whole group (who had their ears on our indirect conversation) also came to know about this.

After I told him, he also replied indirectly.

Somehow, I managed to say him directly (in front of the whole group friends) whatever I wanted to say.

He came and wrote on my hand: a positive reply to my words.

The group end party was so special and precious to me.

*****

After reading some parts of her diary, I closed and kept it in the side. Then I tool out my mobile and called her.

"Hi my princess. Good morning there".

"Hello prince. Good morning, have a great day! What's going there?"

"I have gone through some of your entries".

"My entries?? I am not understanding what are you saying".

"Your diary is with me".

"With you? How?"

"I don't know, I got it in the name of a slam book".

After some seconds of silence

"Oh, oh, it was my problem only, I was in so much hurry (to go home) that I hadn't bothered to look on the cover page".

"So when are you taking it?"

"Come today at my home around 1:00 P.M. I will keep the Slam Book on the window. You will take that and place the diary there only and after keeping it you will be leaving soon from there. I will take it".

“Alright, your Majesty, the same will be done as your wish”.

“Thanks, your highness. Talk to you later”.

CHAPTER 10

During the afternoon, I was along with my friends waiting for the result to be made available by CBSE on their official website. As soon as we were informed that the result is available now, we switched to the CBSE's official website but unluckily we became unable in opening the website for checking our result .A lot of people from all over the country were trying to get their result so there was huge cyber traffic on that website. The weather was also cloudy and it was raining, so there was not a good network signal at all. We still kept on trying by refreshing the same error page more than sixty times and finally we became successful in opening the website.

First of all, we checked Avishek's result by entering his Board's roll no. and date of birth.

After few seconds, we got his result on the window screen, his overall CGPA was 9.2. Then, we checked Shreyansh's result, which was 7.4 CGPA. After him, my result was checked, 8.4 CGPA was my overall marks. Then Animesh and Anurag's result was checked. Animesh had got 8.6 CGPA and Anurag's CGPA was 8.2.

We all were satisfied of our result but we were fearful because we don't know that if our guardians will be satisfied or not with the result we got in Class 10th.

When Shreyansh went to his home and told his guardians about the result, they were satisfied but not much. They told him that if you have scored at least 8.0 CGPA then it would be good, but your this mark, is an average.

When Anurag's parents came to know about his result, they hadn't paid much attention on the marks. They started to have discussion with all the members of his matter on the matters related with the admission to higher classes. Anurag's father told that: Your marks is good, but you could have achieved more than this

Avishek's home:

Avishek's family members were not satisfied at all. His elder brother(M.Tech final year student) scolded him a lot on this matter. His marks were the highest among us, but still his family was not satisfied.

We had also thought that he is going to get good marks (at least 9.6 CGPA) as he was a hard working and an intelligent guy among us.

In Animesh's home:

After hearing the marks, Animesh's parents were happy and satisfied. They congratulated him for what he had achieved. In Class 9th, he got only 7.2 CGPA and then he worked hard, concentrated much on his studies and got 8.6 CGPA, so his family members were happy and satisfied at all. His parents asked him about his wish and in which institution he wants to take admission for Class 12th?

My home:

I had already told my guardians that I'm very sorry for breaking your hopes with me that I'll get a good marks in Class 10th as the truth is that I'm not going to get any good marks at all, my mathematics examination was the worst. After that, from the last two months I had tolerated a lot of scolding and comments from all the sides for the reason that I'm not going to get a good marks in Class 10th, for the reason that I had ruined my career, they were sure that I'm going to fail in mathematics (even I was also worried) but there was a very small believe on myself and my works that I will not be fail in any subject and will surely get at least 7.8 or 8.0 CGPA and due to that small belief, I was patiently waiting for the result. The moment when I got my result, I was glad and really not believing that really I had got 8.4 CGPA. My parents (who had already made themselves satisfied that their son is not going to get more than 7.0 CGPA) were very surprised, they were also not believing.

Then my brother checked my result and showed them in front of their eyes.

After seeing the result they were not only satisfied but happy too. However, 8.4 CGPA was not a very good mark but it was good for me and I was happy because my parents were satisfied with it.

After I got to hear something good from my parents, I felt much free and better, the fear and the trouble was also drained out of my mind .

I went to my room, closed the door, jumped, jumped and danced with much excitement. I thanked God for whatever marks I got.

I came out from the excitement zone, I texted Anamika to know about her results.

8 minutes later, she replied that she had got 9.0 CGPA.

From the next day of the result declaration, each of us started to apply in some different institutions for taking admission in Class 12th with our desired streams.

*****

Admission in Class 12th

For taking admission in Class 12th, we had applied in a lot of institutions and were also preparing for their entrance tests.

Anurag applied for a distance course from a government institution and went to Delhi to get admission in the two year classroom programme of Aakash Institute for the preparation of All India Pre Medical Test (AIPMT).

Animesh was busy in preparing for the entrance tests of various institutions of his area.

Shreyansh went to Ranchi and started preparing to crack the entrance examinations of some institutions located there.

Avishek joined the best Career Institution located in New Delhi for the preparation of Joint Entrance Examination of Indian Institute of Technology (IIT-JEE) along with a distance course of PCM from a private institution.

Anamika was waiting for her BHU's entrance exam results and also she was solving the practice papers deeply in order to give the entrance examinations of some more best schools and colleges as there was a very few seat (most of the seats were reserved for different quotas, the general seat for PCM in Girls Hindu School was only 39 and the candidates were approximately more than five thousands),so the probability of getting selected was very less.

Three weeks later.......

Shreyansh gave six entrance tests of various institutions and in them, he was short-listed by one of the best education providing institution of Ranchi.

Anamika's result also came. Her name was published on 14th position in the merit list of Girls' Hindu School of BHU. Before the result was made available, Anamika had given two more entrance examinations but she became unsuccessful in both of them and then she again, started preparing for the third entrance test then suddenly she got her name in the selection list of BHU.

After being rejected from a lot of institutions due to several reasons, I also got my admission in a private institute at Indore.

Animesh was also selected on the basis of his merit in one of the best school of Haridawar.

The previous month was a very hard time for all of us. We and our parents were also very much worried and disturbed regarding our admission to higher classes.

We all had applied in more than six institutions from all over the country but we were unsuccessful sometimes due to the higher cut off marks of the institution or sometimes due to not passing the entrance examinations.

We kept on trying in giving the entrance exams of some more institutions and finally we were succeed after passing from a lot of difficulties in cracking those tough entrance examination. This time, we became successful, because we worked more and more hard, we practiced a lot and also we have the bad experience of six failures.

[Every person can achieve anything in his life. There's no any barrier to stop them, no failures can stop them if they keep trying and working hard continuously to achieve it. If you have a complete desire, then you will be successful. You can do anything].

CHAPTER 11

After taking admission, all of us came back to our hometown as the new session and the class was going to start from the 4th of July. So, each of us will be leaving our hometown from the end of this month and will set to different cities (too much far from each other).

Just like before, Animesh will be living in Haridawar. Anamika will shift to Varanasi and she'll be staying in the Girls' Hostel of Central Hindu Girls School (CHGS of BHU),I will be setting in Indore, Shreyansh will move to Ranchi, Avishek and Anurag will live in Delhi (at two different places almost 70 kilometres away from each other).

As we were about to get separated from each other and living in different places, so we planned to arrange and celebrate our Farewell and the last meeting with each other.

We did a lot of planning in order to make our FAREWELL party: a happiest memory. This party was only between among the five of us and we had not invited any girl as that party will be only personally for we boys (as after that we will meet each other at the end of the year or more than that: We were not confirmed that when we are going to meet the next).This party was for the best friendship among the five of us which we came holding from the previous four years.

21st July 2016

Hotel Evergreen, Near Station Road

We had booked a ceremony hall (of the hotel) in which everything was arranged according to our planning. Also, we hired a waiter who can serve us and provide the facllities we want. There was also a small place which was a bit higher than the ceremony hall, we told the waiter (who was standing there before our arrival) to place the table and the cake there only and also to add a background music.

After the waiter did all of his works, we went at that place and then five of us together completed the cake cutting procedure. We also shared our cake with the waiter and when then when almost half of the cake was left, we destroyed throwing it at each other and also stamping it on each other faces. We were so much blind that time (during the so much great enjoyment mood) that the waiter also got his face attacked by us.

At the washroom, when we were washing our faces, the waiter was also there.

Anurag and Shreyansh went and apologized with the waiter.

"There's no need to apologize. I can understand", he said to us.

We became relaxed and thanked the waiter for understanding us.

As it was our last meeting, so each of us wanted to hear some words from the mouth of our best friends regarding the life, career, friendship and their future goals.

Animesh turn came first. A small distance from us, he went and started to speak by standing up on that small place (which seems like a small stage):

First of all, I want to tell you guys something from the very beginning of my life at Bettiah. When I came here, there was no one in my circle and also no any person who knows me. I was totally empty and at that moment, I never thought that I will be merged in such a good friendship among the nice people. I was unknown for all of you but still you people never made me feel that I am an unknown person or an outsider. So thank you very much guys for bringing me as a friend in your life.

(We were hearing to him, keeping our all the feelings and the emotions hidden inside us at that moment).

Now, let me tell you something about my life and my desire: Though my life is beautiful but it is more complex too. It makes me feel too unfortunate of myself when I see some people who got the same thing easily which I had got after doing months and months of patience and hard work for it and sometimes I also became unable to get that with doing all the sacrifice which I'm able to do. These kind of situation had happened with me a lot of times and I now I have a habit of tolerating all these things .I only believe on doing the things which is in my hand and never make my mind on the things which is not in my hand what I do is only a self believe that I am going to get it. Sometimes it works and sometimes it doesn't.

About my desire: I wish to become a best Marine Engineer and I'll make every effort in reaching to that profession. I am going part by part. Currently, my desire is to achieve a distinction marks in Class 12th.

I don't know what will happen with me in the future but I'll focus on completing every step, every part to get what I desire. Thank you.

Animesh came out of there and sat among us.

We spend the next few minutes in deciding that who's going the next: Avishek became ready and went on to speak.

Hello friends, once again. Congratulations for the completion of four years of friendship. Just like you all, I am also glad to be a part of our group.

Now here's a very hard time of my life, I want to share with all of you.

Seven years ago, when I came to the new school, nobody wanted to join with me after I got failed in the first examination I gave in that school.

According to the marks, I was at the last position in that class. A lot of people (from that class) make fun of me regarding this issue, they also call me a failure, foolish and some other words related with this. The teachers also told me to concentrate on my studies, even my father was also called a lot of time regarding this issue. They made an indirect comment on my father regarding me. I felt very bad at that time. As I was a small boy, I was knowing(at that times) that study and examination has no value but the moment when they made comment in front of my father, then I realized that It's the value and the prestige of my father. In order to save it, I started making my interest in it and that's how my level in the class started increasing gradually.

Some months later, I came to know that Study is not only a prestige and value, it is everything and without it, we are nothing. I tried to create more and more interest in my studies because I wanted to gain something (I don't know what as I was smaller) but I wanted it.

One year later, my name was called off in the Annual Function of my school and then they awarded me for getting the Second Position in Classroom.

Next day of that, they called my father and gave him more respect, they also congratulated him. Three years later of that, I met one person and was inspired by him to become an IT engineer, which is my mission now.

So that was the turning point of my life and also the moment when a huge change came in my life. I know it was a boring stuff for you, but that was all which I wanted to share with you friends. Thanks for listening.

He ended up. After him, Shreyansh stood up and went there.

Hi guys. Thank you for sharing a best friendship with me. In the past few years, we all came through a lot of problems and bad situations associated with our life. Do you know why we crossed it successfully? We never left each other. I will never forget the moment which was the worst part of my life. When that girl left me, I was completely destroyed and heart-broken but still after some time I managed to live without her and now I'm so much capable that there will be no effect on me if any girl will leave me, break up with me or forget me. The reason is, you guys.

When I was a child, I went to roam in my town fair. I stopped at one shop because I found a toy which attracted me a lot, I wanted to get that toy. When my father came tired from his work, I requested him for this. We both walked to the market. When we reached the shop, the toy was not found there. It was sold, I became sad and upset. The shop owner showed us a lot of other toys but I was not looking any of it. My mind was still on that toy only. So without buying any toys, we had to come out of the town fair.

However, there was a lot of lying in my home but I wanted that toy also, so I went into the town fair again and searched that toy in almost all the near shops. I tried explaining a lot (to the shop owners) about the look and the design of the toy, but I hadn't got it. I still walked on visiting some more shops (nearby) and finally I got that toy. It was hanged in front of a shop just opposite to where I was studying. I reached that shop and spent no time in losing it.

That was my past, which I still remembered and will be remembering forever. From that day till today, I always try more and more to get the things whatever I wanted but I never changed my way by accepting other things in place of it. There are a lot of opportunities in this world so we must be trying in each and everything without wasting time. Who knows if some person has the same thing you want, if one opportunity is waiting for you to come and get it?

Now, I only run behind a single thing and I gave away almost everything, every hope, work or whatever I can do to get it which is a good position in the department of Computer Science. This is my goal and I will not wait for anything until and unless I achieved it. Thank you.

When Shreyansh came back on his place, I went there and began to speak whatever I wanted to say a last message or some important things for my friends.

Dear Friends, thanks for bringing this friendship in a very good stage. First of all, I want to make you understand that there will be no effect on our friendship due to living too much far from each other and there is no doubt in saying that this friendship among us will be on the same position.

Today, I want to share something about the very reality of life. When we will be nothing then the whole society will not respect us, even our family will also not give us any importance. When we cross this situation, nobody wants to listen our problems and help us. This time, a lot of people do some illegal things, which they never wanted to do but they have to do it. Why anybody does suicide? They do it because they feel there is no reason to live their life after they were broken or unable to tolerate the problems of life or when the lose support from their closer ones. The problems and the bad situation are common in every one's life and every people are suffering from different different problems in this world. For that very people, I want to create a reason again in their life through the motivational speaking. I want to make them so much powerful to accept the problems and fight with it. They will be successful, everyone will be successful If they focus on the solutions and not the problems. If the problem has come, then the solution will be also there. We need to find it. Had you ever noticed that how much a problem can make you learn? After passing through each problem of life, we learn a lot about it. It also makes us stronger and that is what which makes things going good. It makes us successful.

I am passing through many problems and difficulties and also I've gone through many of it but I never stopped. I don't want the things which happened in my life, to be happened with anyone and if it will happen then I will be there to make them able to fight with it. This is the commitment with myself. I want to bring a change in the lives of people through my motivational speeches.

For being a motivational speaker, I need to do something great in my life. I will have to achieve a good level to inspire peoples. I also want to do a lot more in my life and I know problems will come and I'm ready to face them.

Best of luck for your upcoming life. Thank you very much.

I ended my speech and then focused on the speech of Anurag : Greetings to all my friends. Today I am very happy because even after crossing all the difficulties, we all are together. In the last years, a lot of people came in our life and a lot went far from our life, but we remained the same five friends. So thanks for this.

There is not something interesting or any special event which happened in life, I have not something special but I wanted to tell you something related with my target of life. I want myself to be represented as a Doctor and I know how difficult the way is for this, but nothing is easy to do, It is us which makes the things easy but for making it easy, we need to sacrifice a lot for that. For me, having an MBBS qualification is my first goal. I'm very interested in Medicals.

Besides this, I also want to contribute in social works but only after I will complete my studies and become a doctor. Currently, I am not focusing much on this as it's the second thing I wanted to do, the first one is to serve as a doctor in the society.

I would like to give answer of a question –Why I wanted to do social works?

There is a lack of awareness among people in our country about many things which they need to know the most. Half of the country's problem can be solved but only If we create the awareness among all the people of our country. Public Awareness in a lot of things, firstly about the Nature: we are destroying us and it is destroying us.

There is also importance of awareness in the cleanliness of the society. We keep a lot of care and cleanliness in our home, but we don't care how our surrounding is. This is also the main reason of why many people suffering from various dangerous diseases. When there will be awareness among them, when they will know about the harmful effects of this on them then this will not happen.

Except this, there are a lot more things I wanted to do, combining all this lack of society, I will be setting social service and also create awareness through my own Non-Government Organization (NGO) which I wish to open.

I want to spread the changes in my areas through the organization. Let us see what happens in the near future.

"Will you guys be helping to social works and awareness through my NGO?

"Yes bro, we will", we all replied.

"So here I end my words. Thanks a lot guys".

When the whole speech was over, we all sat on the round table for having the lunch.

Minutes later: Before we were about to leave, we did some Masti and Hungama for the next of an hour and that's how this "Best Friendship Farewell Party" ended up leaving behind a lot of memories and also a feeling of separation.

When we came out from the Hotel, we shacked hands and hugged each other happily during the last moment of our interaction.

CHAPTER 12

Five days later

Anamika (who was very angry with me) was not replying of my messages. When I called her, I got no response. In the next of some minutes, she had not responded to almost eight of my calls and picked the ninth call.

As soon as the call was received (by her) I said extremely sorry to her for breaking some of her heartily wishes. She wasn't responding to me like before and speaking in the same manner (which tells that she hadn't excused me and still feeling the same).

"I am very sorry for breaking your wishes. I can understand how a person feels wh en his wishes are broken ",I said.

"It's ok", she replied and the call was dropped.

After some minutes, a text message arrived on the phone.

Anamika: I am sitting in between my parents now, talk to you later.

Me: Ok and thanks for forgiving me

No response came from her side.

50 minutes past, I called her (again).

"Hello", I said.

"Hi".

How are you feeling?", I asked in order to make sure that she had excused me or not.

"I'm fine".

(I was glad as she had not talked or mentioned anything related with the previous issue: It was confirmed that she had excused me).

“So what are you doing now?”

“Nothing. When will you leaving for Indore?”

“There are hardly any seat available in any train these days. I think ,I will be going after 6-10 days or more than that and you? When are you going to Varanasi?”

“29th of July”, she replied.

“Just three more days in Bettiah”.

“Hmmm ….but still you don’t want to meet me for the last time”.

“Anamika ….I had never told that”.

“Are we meeting?”

“Yes”.

“When?”

“On 28th of July”.

“Sorry, I will not go that day as I had to do a lot of shopping and also packaging of the things”.

“Ok, tomorrow at 3:00 PM. But, where?

“You tell”.

“Can you come at the Café Delight?”

“Where is it?”

“Near Church Road”.

“Fine. I will be there at the exact time. But you don’t have to be late, otherwise I will move back to the home”.

"If this is so then I will come before 15 minutes and will wait for you".

"You will wait? For me? (surprising) How many minutes?".

"Yes, for you. I will wait for you till your arrival. But why are you asking this? Is this the first time I will be waiting for you?"

"No but what if I came at 3:30 ? Will you be still waiting?"

"Yes, I will be".

"And what If I came after an hour from that time?"

"Then also I'll be waiting but hold on a second. Had you ever waited a single minute for me? Tell me?"

"No, because this kind of situation has never happened"

"No, It was because someone was waiting for you from a longer time".

"Yeah, right. I am sorry".

"It is OK but next time, please don't ask me this that how much I can wait for you and the things related with this."

"Please forgive me for that. I will never ask this again".

"This is not a mistake so stop apologizing. The things revolving inside us need to be cleared. So are you clear that I can wait for you or still there is some problem?"

"No, not any. It is all cleared, and thanks once again for understanding me in a correct way".

"OKAY dear. Can we talk through the Skype Video Calls? My small sister is asking for the mobile now".

"Hmmmm but what your small sister does with your mobile?"

"She play games and listens to some kiddy widdy songs".

“What kind of game she plays? Doesn’t she like to go outside and play games”.

“She wants but she is alone now. Her friend is on a leave. Mostly, she plays games like the Talking Tom, Barbies, Temple Run and more. Do you also play these games”.

“Yes, sometimes ,not always. There are some real life games I enjoy playing”.

“Nice. Let us talk on Skype”.

“Oh, yes, why to make a little kid sad and upset?”

“Right ,right. Thanks.”

(I gave the mobile to my sister who was about to be blasted on me If I have done some more late. I came to my room and opened the laptop. There was a problem within the server which took some large minute time to be fixed and after that I became active on Skype. She was still online waiting for me. She never waited for me on road but on social media she waited a lot for me. I messaged her on the chat box. She replied within seconds. I made a video call and we both resumed talking).

As Anamika told that she will reach exactly at 3:00 PM, so I also planned to reach exactly at the same time by making an estimation of travel time from my home to Church Road but I don’t know how I came three minutes before. Still, I will have to wait for her. I think it is written in my destiny to wait for Anamika ,at whatever time I leave my home I always come minutes before where ever I go to meet her. I never came to know why this happens with me but still I like waiting for her which had become a habit now (on can say).

As there was some minutes in my hand, I went to a shop from where I can watch her coming by and then I’ll go.

When she came and parked her scooty on the side, I came out from the shop but unfortunately, I couldn’t reached to her. It happened because a taxi and a maxi collided with each other. Both the drivers came and then a great fight came in both of them. Fortunately, there was no much damage but the people made a so much crowd that I was unable to go on the other side. The people nearby made the place as a public museum, they were watching and circled the area as if it was not the fight with the drivers but a WWE fight .

I found that If I will be waiting for the crowd to be finished, then it will be too much late so I went inside the crowd (where the fight was going on) and somehow after facing them, I came out.

"Hi. Sorry, I became late today".

"Was it necessary to make me stand here alone for the reason that I had never waited for you? You know how this area is".

"Have you seen what was happening on other side of the road?"

"Yes, I have. So what? You know how much boring and uncomfortable I was feeling here".

"I know it better but what can I do? I myself was on the other side of the road which was too blocked to pass but I still tried to come in between them, do you know how?"

"You were on the other side? I'm so sorry for that".

"Yes, but once again let me tell you that I personally don't want you (or any girl) to stand here (in this crowded place) and wait for me".

"Ok, ok, fine. Come on now, let's get inside the cafe."

*****

Café Delight

Church Road

"Why are you so sad? Is there anything wrong with you?"

"Yes, can you describe how fast the time went on and made us stand here, from which we are going far away".

"Time never slows down for anyone but don't be sad Anamika, it's just a matter of two days".

"Two years? How easy is it to say. And what do you think after that we will be together? No, we will be more far than this".

"Wherever we will go, we will be interacting during the vacations. Shouldn't you'll be coming to Bettiah?"

"I will be coming but what if the destiny doesn't allow us to meet again?"

"Destiny is not of a much importance for me. If both want to go together, then surely we will meet again. Nobody can stop us but if we don't want then nobody can make us to meet".

"Would you like to go together with me? Would you like to meet me again?"

"Yes, yes, yes. Do you still have some negative thoughts regarding this?"

"No, just I want to make my heart clear in this very last moment of ours".

"Whenever you are mentioning this "last" I am going in doubt that is it really the last meeting of our life?"

"No, I'm sorry for mentioning it".

"Alright. So, please change your mood and be happy. If there will be any problem, then we will sort it out together".

"No Abhijeet, there's no any problem but can you please once again make me believe that we will be close with each other ,no matter how far we go".

I closed my eyes and kissed her for more than a minute.

"Is it the need to make you believe? Don't you have a trust on our relationship?"

"I do have but we never went too much far from each other and so I am worried a little".

"Don't worry. I make my promise not to break this relationship no matter how many problems and situations or bricks lie between it".

(She hugged me. Her sadness got changed into happiness but not much).

"So, what will you do? I'm also worried a little about you".

"What happens when bricks from a vehicle accidently fall on the road making it blocked from both of the sides of the National Highway?"

"Those bricks were thrown as soon as possible otherwise there will a huge traffic".

"The same I will do with the problems coming in between our relationship. I'll break it and throw all of it".

"Great, great. If the bricks were the problems coming in our life then what was the National Highway".

"It was the road of our relationship, stupid".

"Ok. Now you see there are a lot of people we meet in our life and a lot of products we see and use in our daily life. Whenever anybody gets the better product than the older one, then he leaves it and switches to the new one".

"I can understand the true thing which you wanted to say for me".

"What?"

"However, it will hurt me a lot but I'll somehow manage to stay alone".

"No, you had not understood that. I wanted to ask that can you be happy with the one which you have now or you will go on to other? Whatever I am, I'll be incomplete if this ever happened. "

"Don't think this, Abhijeet. It is not going to happen. I am already happy with you and also I love you a lot. So I don't need any better guy other than this, I need you only. You will be staying forever with me".

"Thanks for making me understand. I Love you".

(She closed her eyes and hugged me even more tight).

"You are the best part of my life".

"You also".

"Aacha, Abhijeet, tell me where will you live in Indore? Do you have any relative there?"

"No, I had already booked a room attached with everything, just like a hotel, but it's an apartment".

"Is it a family apartment or the Bachelors?"

"It's a family apartment but two top rooms are for the Bachelor's in which I'll be living in the one and on the other room, two engineering students (who are friendly brothers) are living there."

"So where will you have the food? Will you make it by yourself or from the hotel?"

"No, dear. There will be not that much time with me to cook. I will switch to monthly planning of any mess nearby who will provide best services".

"Do you know how to cook foods?"

"Yes, but not that much capable to make it daily. Do you?"

"No, I only know How to boil the milk and make a tea".

"Then in this case, I'm far much better than you".

"Hmmm. From where had you practiced to make food?"

"Whenever my mother comes late from her work then me and my brother together used to cook food, mostly we are related with the non – veg".

"Wow, nice support to your Mother. But you hadn't told me about the beginning of this cooking?"

"It all started from a normal day. My Dad and Mother were late in the office. We, both brothers, then decided to make Chicken and Rice by ourselves as it.

It was our mood to make it on that day. We have seen our mother cooking in the kitchen, so we did the same processes as our Mother does".

"How was the food then?"

"It was good. We both liked what we had made. From that day, we continued to improve ourselves".

"It's great that you both became independent (from that day) for making something as per the wish".

"Yes and how about you?"

"I'm uneducated in this".

"What a fun is it? You need to learn how to cook it otherwise it will be a problem in my future".

"What's the connection between your future and my cooking?"

"You will never understand".

"I know, I know. Don't worry, I'll learn it someday".

"I am not telling you this because of work in the kitchen, I'm telling it because the society will make a fun of you, regarding this problem".

"Yes, yes, it is right. I'll take care about the credits of my family".

"Thanks for that. So what are your nearest goals?"

"After six years, I'll convince my Dad and my Mom making a request telling them about my heart desires".

"I'm not asking about the marriages, dear, I'm asking about the educational goals".

"Sorry, actually the same matter was going on so I thought you were asking about that only".

"But I liked whatever you said. So will you really go and ask your parents regarding this?"

"Yes, yes. The things will be much more different in the next coming years. But by the way what will you do for this?"

"I haven't decided it, yet. I'll tell you when the right time will come".

"Alright, alright, fine. Let's wait for right time".

"Yes, tell me something about your career plans from now?"

"After doing 10+2 , I will be taking admission in a better college for studying Civil Engineering. When I'll complete Graduation then I'll come back and join a well-established job".

" Hmmmm Hhmmm. Civil engineers ?"

"And what's happening with your future goals? Planned anything?

"To pass Class 12 with good marks, then to do Bachelor of Business Management (BBM) and Master Of Business Administration (MBA) from a best faculty colleges. After this, I will work for some years as an employee and then will think of setting my own business when I'll be capable of investing".

"You will be having six years of study after Class 12th. Is Post Graduation important?"

"It totally depends on the choice and also on the goal setting of any person".

"All of the best for that. Can we have some fruit juice? I'm feeling thirsty".

"Sure, please hold on a minute".

(I went to the counter and bought out two fruit juice bottles).

"I wish if we had met in a restaurant, then we have every item and some more options", I said (after coming back from there).

"No problem, dear, sit. It is all fine here and also I don't want to go again in the restaurant, we went there a lot of times but we never came here".

"Yeah,yeah. So would like to come with me in the city park?"

"No,not there. I want to visit the park, which is inside the temple campus".

"As you wish then let us go there".

We were sitting on a bench in the temple park and the weather was too cloudy and cool. We had decided to take each other's photograph of this awesome time spent with each other.

After having those wonderful moments spent with each other, we were on the way back to the homes.

While we were too much far from our homes, the heavy rainfall became likely to come. We decided to go back to a safer place. The best safe place we saw, was the Temple.

Both of us came inside the ground floor of the temple and kept watching the rain, wishing it to stop, but that rain seemed to be unstoppable.

(The rainfall had always been a great indicator of my life. It often falls and strikes my way whenever something better or the worse is going to happen in my life. I am watching this whole rainfall existence in my life from my childhood days only).

For the next twenty minutes, we remained sitting and talking with each other, sadly. (Yes, we both were sad at that time, because soon after some minutes we will be separated in two roads).

A few minutes past, the rain couldn't stop, but slowed down. We came out from the temple and began to reach fast to our homes.

(We both were sad, very sad in the way, but still we ended, smiling and looking happily towards each other with some of the finest talks and ever so best hug and sweet kisses).

CHAPTER 13

Eight days later, I went to Indore travelling in Rajendra Nagar-Indore Express from Patna Junction. It took me 23 hours and 30 minutes to reach the destination. After coming to Indore Junction, I had to take a taxi for Chattrapati Nagar which consumed more than twenty minutes.

From Chattrapati Nagar, I walked in the way of the apartment which was few meters away.

After three hours, I settled everything inside the room and then after that I went to have a food and do registration in the nearby mess with one of my flat mate who is a bit older than me.

The classes were about to start from the next three days, so during that gap of days, I thought of making a good turn with my flat mates so that they can support and help me whenever it will be needed. Both of them were nice persons ,so it hadn't took a long time in getting attached with them.

Each day, three of us walk together to go in the mess, we went to visit some awesome places, enjoyed together and moreover they also shared each and everything of the city which was necessary to know in order to get rid from the future problems.

P.S. Institute of Commerce

The first class at P.S. Institute of Commerce

Today is my first class in this new college and I was very much excited because of that. I had unattended the class since a week due to the reservation problems but now I will be attending it.

On the very exact of the college time, I reached to my class. I was then connected and interacted by my colleagues who were very funny and friendly too. I was talking with the boys colleagues and also asking about the studies of the college. The girls of my class were staring at me as if I was the odd one out or I belong from the another planet. It was making me feel a little uncomfortable.

When the Professor came in the classroom, everybody became silent.(Our class was a college class but the atmosphere and the discipline was just like a school).

The Professor had his eyes on me. As he was the English Professor, he called me to give an English speech on any topic of my choice.

Before I could think something to make some excuses, he directed me to stand on the class stage.

I became nervous but as there was no any option left, so I started to speak about some matters of my life and began to speak it as a motivational speech to give my first impression on the unknown colleagues and also on the English Professor.

Good morning, everyone. This side is Abhijeet, standing by your side to give a speech.

As you all know, today is my first day here, so let me tell you something about myself and my life before I came here.

From the very beginning, I had decided that I will study commerce but when the results became available, the closer ones told me to go with Science saying that Commerce isn't good.

But for someone who is interested in it, Commerce is everything for them.

From the past few years ,I had faced almost a lot of problems similar to this in which people want me to go in another direction, but I never listened to them and this is reason why I'm here today. I have never done the things what others told me to do. I always tried to get what I want, I always do the things which I wanted to do and I'm getting it and

doing it, because of a very simple reason, never to gave up the self wishes and to try continuously for it.

My very current wish is to do everything I will have to do to be in a good position in the field of Commerce and after that I want to serve in this society as a public motivational speaker.

My intro is finished now, but I want to say something related with failures- May I speak it ,Sir? (The professor nodded)

There is no doubt in saying that there are a lot of failures in life but we don't know that after crossing all these failures, we gain experience to handle it, we gain correct knowledge about it and both of these things are inexpensive. These both can give us everything we want to have, these both can make us successful.

Once, only once, If we have made our mind to get anything we like, then we will be getting it, surely. Failures will also come but there's no need to be afraid because of that, we will fight with all the failures, we will cross it and then we will stand up again being much more stronger than before. Nobody can make us fall again, only we can stop ourselves from reaching the destination- fear stops us, let us overcome this fear and try to look forward directly on our ambition. Let us work smart to get the things in which we have made our mind. One day, you will definitely reach to the destination.

Thank you so much for listening such a long time taking speech ,thank you so much. That was what which I want to share between everyone because I had felt it in my own life. Thank you so much, let's do our best in reaching our goals.

(The speech ends)